# DARK WORLD

### The Xandra #8

## HERBERT GROSSHANS

# PROLOGUE

ICEWORLD, THE FIFTH PLANET CIRCLING AN ALIEN SUN 300 LIGHT-YEARS from Earth, is a savage world of high, rugged mountains, vast plains with tall grasses, wild forests, and long, wide rivers snaking through flat lands and mountains that empty their turbulent waters into huge, deep lakes. There is only one ocean. It is as rough and unfriendly as the land.

The weather on Iceworld is unpredictable, with great temperature fluctuations between seasons that are twice as long as the seasons on Earth. It is a world plagued by vicious thunderstorms, hurricanes and torrential rains in the summer and by violent snowstorms in the long winter when the snow never seems to stop falling.

One would think that nothing could survive on such a planet, but when humans set up a research station in a somewhat moderate area in the Western Hemisphere they discovered Iceworld was inhabited by ferocious beasts and a race of intelligent savages, who called themselves the Sras.

They also discovered that humans were not the only intruders into this wild world. Explorers from a race of space faring aliens became stranded 1,000 years before the humans set up their station. Their descendants had grown in numbers and spread across large areas of the planet. They were the Jnaar and had grown nearly as savage as the Sras.

The Sras and the Jnaar were sworn enemies.

Both races live much of the time in the underground tunnels and giant caverns below the surface of Iceworld. Only during the summer do they send out hunting parties to gather wild grains and hunt for meat.

The humans live inside a huge artificial habitat that looks like a giant egg. It protects the humans from the violent weather outside.

Thirty-five humans make this artificial world their home; seventeen men and eighteen women. Originally there had been 39 men and women, but four are missing. Rob Cameron, Rudi Malone, and Irwin Hunter went into the subterranean world to search for Regina Seagul, an abducted xenologist. Their guides, Raaskar, a Jnaar male, and his mate, Laneea, and their daughter Raas-ini, led them to one of the underground Jnaar cities, where they hope to engage the help of the Jnaar in their search for the missing woman.

# CHAPTER ONE

THE SNOW ALMOST TOUCHED THE BOTTOM OF THE GIANT EGG-LIKE structure that was the habitat of the humans on Iceworld. The snow had stopped falling, but the sky was as cloudy as ever.

Inside the habitat, Valissa, Rob's fiancée, sat at a table with her friends Teresa and Holger Schreiber, speculating what the three men, who had gone into the underground tunnels in search of Regina Seagul, were doing.

"They've been gone nearly a month," Valissa said. "I wish Rob had stayed here. I miss him and feel lonesome without him. He said they'd try to send messages, but he suspected it might not be possible. The rocks would probably prevent any signals from getting through."

"It seems he was right about that because we haven't heard from them." Teresa put her hand over Valissa's in a gesture of friendship. "Don't worry so much. I'm sure they're okay." She gave Valissa an encouraging smile. "You're not alone. I'm here for you and so is Holger."

Valissa wiped her nose with the back of her hand and sniffed. "I know and I appreciate it, but you can't replace Rob when I sleep alone in my bed at night."

"I'm alone at night too, honey. Too bad that big hunk of a man, you know who I'm talking about, was so damned reserved. Who would have thought a man like that had so many inhibitions? I would have given him a good time."

Teresa laughed heartily. "He would have remembered my great passion as he's sleeping in those dark, cold tunnels without a woman embracing his hard, muscular body."

Schreiber, the man with them, snickered. "I'm glad I don't have all these sexual hang-ups. Must be a drain on your system."

"Well, Holger, my friend, somehow I can't believe that you don't have any sexual desires. You can't be dead down there, and I don't really want to know how you relieve your anxieties, which I have no doubt you have. So you're not attracted to women. You like men. Tell me, did you ever have the hots for another man?"

"I had. A long time ago." He seemed reluctant to answer her.

"Can't be that long ago. You're not so old. Was he your lover?"

Schreiber nodded as a faraway look clouded his dark eyes. "For a short time only."

"Did you have a sexual relationship with him?" Teresa sounded almost like an interrogator. Schreiber didn't answer. "Did you?"

"What do you think?" Schreiber's eyes flashed angrily.

His reaction surprised Valissa. She had never seen him angry. He was usually calm and in control of his emotions.

Teresa slapped his shoulder with a jovial laugh. "So you did have a little taste of heaven, you sly dog. Perhaps if the right man came along you would discover feelings you thought were dead. That's how I felt with Malone, believe it or not. He may look like a huge ogre to you, but I found him ruggedly handsome."

"Why didn't you tell him that?" Schreiber seemed to have regained his composure. "You have nobody to blame but yourself if you feel like you've missed having his sweaty body laboring on top of yours."

"You make it sound like something dirty. I'd call it making passionate love."

"Call it what you will. You should have made the first move when you noticed he didn't have the guts to romance you." Schreiber took a swig from his coffee mug. "Now you may never get the chance."

"Why shouldn't I?"

"He may get lost in those underground tunnels and not come back."

"Don't be so negative," Teresa chided him and motioned with her head

4

toward Valissa. "Of course he'll be back. They'll all come back safe and sound."

"And soon," Valissa said. "I hope they find that woman, otherwise it'll all have been for nothing." She rose from her seat. "See you at lunch. I'm going to do my exercises." She smiled at them both. "I don't want to be fat and out of shape when Rob comes back."

"No chance of that happening, unless you get yourself pregnant by one of the men who have been ogling you and who would like nothing better than to get into those tight pants you're wearing." Teresa heaved a loud sigh. "You eat like a bird and you seem to spend most of your time in the exercise room. I wish I had the drive and the desire to be so disciplined." She touched her belly. "I have to get rid of this little ring I've noticed lately. I wish I had a man to exercise with. It's so much more fun."

Holger shook his head. "Like I said...sexual hang-ups."

"They're not hang-ups, Holger." It was Teresa's turn to be annoyed. "Those feelings are called desires. Every normal person has them."

Valissa walked away, suddenly not interested in the conversation of her friends. She had to admit, Teresa and Holger were the only people she associated with on a regular basis. In the beginning she had chummed a little with the two sisters Naomi and Gabriella Lewis, but they were spending more and more time with Teresa's sons, Sigmund and Conrad. The four of them were Valissa's age, but she felt like a fifth wheel whenever she sat with the two couples, which happened less and less frequently.

As for the men who were ogling her, according to Teresa, she wasn't unaware of them. Did they really think just because Rob wasn't around she'd jump into bed with them?

She wasn't that desperate for sex, unlike Teresa, who talked about sex all the time. Most of the men were too old for her anyway, except Sigmund and Conrad, and they only had eyes for Naomi and Gabriella, which is how it should be.

She went back to her room and changed into her exercise outfit, a tight, formfitting bodysuit that left her legs and arms bare. Since she always felt somewhat naked wearing it, because it revealed every detail of her slim figure, she threw a thin cape over her shoulders. When she entered the exercise room, there was only one other person in there. She recognized Wong. He was busy lifting weights. Valissa went to one of the treadmills and started running. Watching Wong, she had to admit it was obvious he lifted weights on a regular basis. His naked upper body rippled with muscles.

If it weren't for her engagement to Rob, she might even have made a play for Wong. He was an attractive man.

She chided herself for even thinking it, but thoughts were not deeds. Besides, she had seen him in the company of that sex-goddess Cara Gunn. Nobody could compete with her. There were certain rumors going around about Cara and some of the men, and Valissa had no trouble believing there might be some truth to those rumors.

Wong appeared to be finished with his weightlifting. He came over to take the treadmill beside Valissa. "Trying to stay in shape?" he gave her a friendly smile.

She nodded without slowing her pace. "There's nothing else to do around here," she said, raising her voice to make herself heard over the droning of the treadmill. "I need to be physically active to stay healthy. You know what they say: A healthy body is a healthy mind." She smiled. "I don't want to look into the mirror and close my eyes because I hate to see my out-of-shape lumpy body."

"The way you look there's no danger you'll have to close your eyes." He moved his eyebrows up and down and grinned, like a teenage boy trying to impress a girl he admires with a flattering statement but covering it up by making it sound funny.

Her face felt flushed, the way it always did when a man gave her a compliment about the appearance of her body. The strict religious rules her parents imposed on her when she grew up still lingered inside her subconscious mind, even though she tried hard to be more open and cast away the shackles the religion of her parents put on her. She could still hear her mother. "A woman should not display her body to a strange man. Only her husband should see her unclothed."

Unclothed also meant no tight bodysuits, like the one she wore right now while exercising. However, her parents and their religion were millions of kilometers away, on another planet. They would never again dictate what she should wear or how she should behave. The feeling of freedom was great but she also felt homesick. She missed the love she had shared with her family.

She looked up when she heard Wong talking.

"Did I violate some kind of taboo with what I just said?"

She shook her head. "No, you didn't. It's been a while since a man complimented me on my looks. I mean other than my fiancé Rob. It's just...I remembered what my parents kept telling me, that's all."

"Where are your parents?"

"On Nu-Eden. They're farmers. I just realized I'll never see them again. Ever."

"Perhaps you will. You can't lose hope."

"I have no such illusions. Even though the Xandra promised not to turn the second wave of settlers into her creatures, including some of the people from the first wave, the ones she left unchanged. My family was among the lucky ones; at least they were when I left Nu-Eden. But can you trust the Xandra? She's an alien entity and thinks on different levels than us humans."

"I only know about the Xandra from what I was told, so I can't comment. Is she really so powerful and has the ability to create clones from living people and transfer their minds into these clones? Can she actually influence people's minds?" Wong slowed the speed of his treadmill and let it come to a halt.

He stepped off the belt and moved in front of Valissa's machine. She reasoned he did that so he could look directly at her without craning his neck. It also gave him a better view of her body, making her self-conscious again.

"I experienced what she can do first hand," she said, remembering her first sexual encounter with Rob. At the time she thought it was nothing but a lucid dream, until she found out differently. Both, she and Rob, had been under the spell of the Xandra. She had done things she'd never do while conscious and awake and in control of what she said and did. As she thought about those things, she felt her cheeks heating up again. She wiped her hand across her forehead.

"I am getting hot from this vigorous exercise," she said breathlessly, trying to cover up her embarrassment.

"You don't have to exercise to look hot," Wong said, giving her his boyish grin again.

His remark didn't help. She laughed nervously. "Are you flirting with me, Mister Wong?"

"Mister Wong?" He tilted his head, his expression serious. "My name is Len. Don't call me Mister. It makes me feel old." He chuckled. "It is not difficult to flirt with you. I'm sure all the unattached men, perhaps even some attached ones, have flirted with you. You're a beautiful girl."

She reduced the speed of her treadmill but kept walking at a slower rate. "I'm also engaged to a wonderful man who I love with all my heart."

"I know, but Rob isn't here."

"That still doesn't mean I'm forgetting about him. I'm certain he is not forgetting about me, either. Our love is probably the only thing helping him to endure what he is going through at this moment. Who knows what kind of awful things he has to face." She gave Wong a challenging look. "He is a very brave man and doing what most men on the Station were afraid to do."

"I'm not going to challenge your statement because you're right, Rob is a brave man. I question his motives for going, though. He didn't even know Regina. Why did he go into unknown danger to search for a woman who means nothing to him? Why did he leave you alone?"

Valissa stepped from the treadmill, silent for a moment. How could she answer Wong's question when she didn't know the answer herself? Why did Rob leave her alone with all these strangers?

"I guess he's concerned about other people's welfare. Back on Nu-Eden he went to search for my sister-in-law after she ran away into the jungle when nobody else cared to follow her. He's just that kind of a man."

"I would never have done that if you were my fiancée," Wong insisted in pursuing the subject. "Like I said, he doesn't even know Regina. Perhaps there were other reasons? Something you're not telling me? Was everything all right between you two?"

"Of course everything was all right. Still is." She felt like shouting at Wong for even suggesting she and Rob might have had problems. "You are right, there was another reason. He wanted to find out more about this Dark Goddess who is supposed to live somewhere underground."

Wong nodded solemnly. "I see. The Sras and the Jnaar talked about an evil entity living in the underground caverns. They called her worshippers Shadow-dwellers. Why would Rob be so interested in an alien goddess?"

"Because she sounds a lot like the Xandra on Nu-Eden. He is worried this Dark Goddess might be the equivalent of the Xandra."

"If she is, what is he going to do about her?" Wong shook his head. "I would think after escaping the influence of one alien entity he would stay far away from anything remotely similar."

"One would think so." Valissa had to agree. She shrugged and heaved a loud sigh. "But that's Rob. I tried to talk him out of it. He wouldn't listen. He told me something is compelling him to find out the truth about this Dark Goddess."

"He sounds like a man driven by something."

"He's not a fanatic, if that's what you mean," Valissa defended Rob.

Wong held up both hands. "I'm not saying that. I've never really spent much time with Rob, so I can't say I know him well. I'm sure he is a competent man and knows what he's doing. Let's hope he survives and comes back safely."

Valissa picked up her cape. "I'm going to hit the showers." Wong's eyes had followed her as she bent to get her cape and she could almost see the disappointment in his face when she covered her upper body with it. "I'll see you around."

"Wait." He reached out with the obvious intention to touch her arm but changed his mind at the last moment. "Listen, Dr. Renaldo and I are taking the Landroamer this afternoon to investigate something in the forest. Jennifer Ratzenberger is also accompanying us. She's a biologist. Would you be interested in coming with us?"

"What are you going to investigate?"

"Some peculiar animals Dr. Renaldo apparently saw. I'm not quite sure."

"Why would you want me along? I know nothing about peculiar animals."

"Neither do I. My specialty is computers not animals." Wong shrugged. "I'm only going along as the driver."

"What would be my function?"

"Your function would be to look beautiful and grace us with your presence." Wong gave her a disarming smile.

She laughed when she saw his innocent expression. "You're making me suspicious. Too many compliments. Will we have to go outside? It's quite cold out there."

"We have the best insulated cold weather suits money can buy. At least they were the best seven years ago when they were purchased. It'll be fun and a change from the daily boring routines. Look at you, exercising every morning, taking a shower, having lunch, spending a boring afternoon watching holograms, sometimes the same ones, or having boring conversations with boring people. Then going for supper, after that a boring evening, and then to bed… alone. The same routine starts the next day. You should jump at the chance to do something different."

Valissa rolled her eyes. "The way you describe my life here sounds even more boring. I'm tempted, but—"

"What?"

"How would it look? I mean…you and I, we aren't really friends who hang out."

"No, we're not, but we could become good friends. In fact, we should, because my best friend, Hunter, is probably bonding with your fiancé. So it only makes sense that you and I also spend some time together."

"You make it sound so logical and simple. And tempting." She was tempted. Life on the Station had become a boring routine, and a change would give her a chance to think of other things besides missing Rob. She nodded, pursing her lips.

"Okay. I'll come with you. As long as there are no strings attached."

"Fine. And don't worry. Nobody expects anything from you as payment, including me. We'll leave shortly after lunch. Meet us in the supply room so we can outfit you with a suit." He looked her up and down. "You are tall for a girl, you know."

"I know. I'm hundred-sixty-five centimeters."

"Like I said…tall. I'm only three centimeters taller."

She chuckled softly. "You're actually short for a man."

Wong pulled a face. "After all the compliments I gave you? Do you have to rub it in?"

"But you're so muscular. It makes you look bigger." As her gaze wandered down his body, she felt her cheeks going red again when she noticed the large bulge in his small, tight briefs.

He's probably big down there, too, by the looks of it. A month without Rob and no sex gave cause for crazy thoughts. "I'll be there," she said, turning and walking away quickly to cover her embarrassment.

"One o'clock," he called after her. "Be there at one o'clock."

As she stood in the shower, she had sudden doubts about going. What would Rob think if he knew what she was about to do?

Then again—what was she actually doing? She was only going on a trip in the Landroamer with three other people. That's all. She wasn't cheating on Rob. She wasn't doing anything wrong.

She made up her mind then and there. She'd go. Suddenly, she looked forward to getting away from the Station for a few hours.

When she told Teresa and Schreiber at lunchtime about it, the older woman raised a delicate eyebrow and smiled enigmatically. "He's a handsome man, that Wong. Missing a few centimeters in height to make him a real hunk, but you could do worse."

"What do you mean by that?" Valissa demanded. "I have no interest in him."

"No? You accepted his invitation."

"He told me himself, there are no strings attached. He just wants to be my friend."

Teresa and Schreiber burst out laughing. "Honey, let me fill you in on what men really want." Teresa bent forward and lowered her voice a little. "Men are not interested in a platonic relationship with a woman, especially one as pretty as you. They may say they are, but all they really want is your pussy. If you're smart and horny enough, you'll let Wong have it. Your man won't be back for months and a healthy young woman like you needs to feel a man inside her once in a while. You need to work up a sweat underneath a man or..." She chuckled. "Or on top of him if you prefer. You'll need to let go of your inhibitions and let your juices flow, or you'll end up suffering from some kind of neurosis. Your body needs to balance those hormones for your mind to stay healthy."

Valissa stared at the older woman. "Are you suddenly some kind of psychiatrist?"

"Actually, I studied to be one before I married my late husband, but mostly I am talking about myself." She sighed and smiled sadly. "It's been quite some time since I had a man moan into my ears while he labors between my clenching thighs. I've always had a strong sex-drive. I have to admit I need a man badly." Her eyes flicked to Schreiber. "The only male friend I have on the Station is not interested in giving me what I want and need. You're lucky, honey, a man wants you and that thing between your legs that makes you a woman. My advice...give it to him. You can only benefit."

Valissa shook her head. "I won't cheat on Rob. I could never forgive myself."

"Give it a couple more months and you'll be climbing the walls. By that time Wong may not be interested in you anymore. He may go back to that black-haired walking pussy Cara Gunn. I've seen them together, and it's obvious what she's giving him."

Schreiber gave a little chuckle. "She's giving him what she's giving every man who wants it."

"Then I have nothing to worry about. Wong gets his sexual satisfaction from Cara, and I'll give him my friendship." Valissa gave Teresa a triumphant smile. "I can live with that."

"What about your sexual satisfaction?"

"That's why I exercise. It keeps my body in shape and my hormones balanced. It keeps me from thinking the wrong thoughts."

"Do you moan during your exercise and scream when you're done?"

"Of course not. Why would I?"

"You would if it made you feel good," Teresa responded. "I moan during the only exercise I prefer and I scream at the end when my partner digs his hands into my buttocks and holds me against him until he's done."

"I never scream," Valissa said, blushing.

"Well, don't feel bad, not all women do," Teresa said. "Some only whimper. Do you at least move and moan a little when you have sex with a man?"

Valissa clenched her fists as she thought of Rob and the pleasure she experienced when they made love.

Of course she moved. She was a passionate woman. She moaned when she had an orgasm, but now she couldn't even remember how it actually was to have one. She felt so alone sometimes and missed Rob terribly. She missed the way he looked at her. She missed his strong arms holding her at night.

"Why are we talking about this?" she mumbled in a low, almost subdued voice.

"Yes, why are we?" Schreiber added.

"Because it's natural to talk about the things we don't have and miss. I'm just trying to give some advice to a friend who seems to need it." Teresa focused on Schreiber. "You and I have become pretty good friends, wouldn't you agree?"

Schreiber nodded. "Yes, we have."

"Don't friends do nice things for each other? Don't friends usually try to make their friends feel good?"

"I suppose so. What are you getting at?"

"Let me put it bluntly. You're a man, on the outside anyway, and you have the equipment to make me feel good. What if I asked you to come to my room and sleep in my bed tonight? Just hold me for a while and use that male equipment of yours to make me happy. Would you do that for a friend? For me? You may even enjoy it."

Schreiber gave her a thoughtful look. "I would do that for you, but my male equipment may not work. Women don't turn me on."

"By the tail of the comet! We don't even have to have the lights on. You could pretend I'm a man. My mouth and my buttocks wouldn't feel any different in the dark from those of a man. You just have to move a little lower with your pleasure maker before you insert it. Where there is a will there is a way."

"Perhaps there is no will."

"I remember you telling Rockwell at the orientation meeting you would consider contributing to the gene pool of our group. How did you think you could achieve that unless you had sex with a woman?" Teresa almost glared at Schreiber, obviously challenging him to give her a reasonable and satisfying answer. "In fact, I also remember you saying it wouldn't be a sacrifice. That means you would enjoy it."

"You're correct. I said that." Schreiber chuckled softly. "I only said it to annoy Rockwell."

"Are you saying you wouldn't enjoy having sex with me?"

Schreiber lifted his shoulders. "I don't know if I'd enjoy it or not. I've never been in that situation."

Teresa put her hand on his in an intimate gesture. "Maybe you should take me up on my invitation and find out," she said with a quiet voice. "If nothing else, you'll spend a night with a friend in the same bed. What harm lies in that?"

"We may not be friend after that. I snore."

Teresa laughed. "So do I."

Valissa looked at the large clock on the wall. "I'd better go. I have fifteen minutes to get ready." She rose and looked around for Wong, hoping to find him at his usual table, but she didn't see him. He was probably already in the supply room getting things ready. She didn't want to be late.

Teresa's eyes were serious. "Think about what I said, Valissa. Grab an opportunity when it comes and don't think too much about it. Follow your feelings and don't suppress your body's desires. If you do, some day they'll overwhelm you and you'll do things you don't want to do but are forced to. Life is like that."

"I'll give everything you said some thought." She walked away quickly, heading for her room.

When she got to the supply room, they were already waiting for her. Dr. Renaldo turned out to be a pleasant man, nearly as short as Wong, with a round face and hair hanging down to his shoulders, but the woman, Jennifer Ratzenberger, seemed a bit aloof at first impression. Quite tall, she towered over both men. Her thin body, narrow face, and her gray eyes, as cold as steel, didn't appear friendly, but when she smiled at Valissa, it lit up her face and eyes.

"So you are Wong's mystery date," Jennifer said.

"Is that what he called it? A date?" Valissa gave Wong a disapproving look.

Wong held up both hands. "In my defense...I never mentioned the word date."

"That's true, he never said date," Jennifer agreed. "I just assumed you were his new girlfriend."

Valissa shook her head. "I'm not that either. I'm engaged to Rob Cameron."

"Isn't that the guy who went with Hunter to look for Regina?" Renaldo inquired.

"That's him."

"I remember now seeing you with him." Jennifer gave Valissa an apologetic smile. "Rumors are that you colonists are supposed to form only a loose relationship in order to keep the gene pool diversified, you know, one woman has children with different men. So I just presumed... I meant no offense."

"That's okay. By the way, my name is Valissa."

"I'm Jennifer. Welcome to our little group. I assume Wong filled you in why we are going on this outing?"

"He did. Apparently, Dr. Renaldo spotted some peculiar animals."

"Not apparently." Renaldo chuckled good-humoredly. "I did see something when I scanned the area a few days ago. Unfortunately, the computer could not enhance the images large enough for me to make out details. What

I think I saw was a flock of large, black birds. They burst from the trees and settled back into the thick branches moments later. Something spooked them, and it would be interesting to discover what kind of animal is roaming the forest in this cold weather, not to mention the birds, if they were birds."

"Here," Wong said, handing Valissa a bundle. "This suit should fit you. Try it on while I look for a pair of boots for you."

Valissa unfolded the bundle and noticed it was the same type of cold weather suit she wore when they left the space shuttle that brought them to this planet. When she slipped into it, she discovered it fit her perfectly, unlike that other one. Wong brought a pair of insulated boots. They also felt comfortable when she put them on.

The others were already dressed in their outfits. They had, obviously, been waiting for her.

"I'm ready," she said, not wanting to be the one holding them back.

"Good. So are we." Renaldo looked at Wong. "How about all the stuff I requested?"

"Already stowed away safely on the Roamer."

"Well, let's go then." Renaldo grabbed a small backpack and threw it across his shoulder. "We don't have too much time. I don't want to get caught in the dark coming back."

Valissa had never been inside the Landroamer and was surprised how roomy and comfortable it was inside. Wong drove it into the elevator. When the doors opened again, he eased it out of the tower onto the snow outside. The Landroamer slid silently across the solid blanket of snow as they headed for the distant forest.

She was still a little apprehensive about going on this trip, but when she looked out of the rear window at the giant egg floating above the white snow, she was happy to have accepted Wong's invitation. She had been cooped up far too long inside the research station that more and more seemed like a prison to her than a refuge from the harsh elements.

# CHAPTER TWO

THE SECOND OF THE RUNNERS RETURNED WITH A NEGATIVE REPORT. NOBODY in the two settlements the runners visited had heard about a strange woman having been brought from the outside.

Cameron and his companions sat in the backyard of Raaskar's home discussing the last runner's account.

"It doesn't mean she isn't here," Malone mused. "I wish we could do our own investigation instead of sitting here on our butts doing nothing, waiting for all the runners they sent out to come back. I'm going stir-crazy with all this inactivity."

"This is the best way," Hunter argued. "We should be grateful to the Jnaar for doing this. We'd only get lost in the giant maze of tunnels and caverns and end up finding nothing. A pure waste of time."

"Those other inhabited caverns must be quite a distance away," Cameron said. "We've been here close to two months now and only two of the runners came back. I agree with Malone about going stir-crazy."

"At least we have a safe place to stay and we can't complain about the food the Jnaar are providing us. In addition to other benefits." Hunter grinned when Cameron raised an eyebrow.

"Speak for yourself," Cameron said. "We don't get any benefits." Except for that one-time experience with Carini. Strange, He hadn't been able to find her anywhere. He couldn't get her out his mind. Even thinking about Valissa didn't help. Not for the first time did he feel guilty when he thought about that mysterious girl who had come out of nowhere and disappeared the same way.

He hadn't mentioned the incident with the Jnaar girl he met and had sex with on the second day after their arrival in the underground city of the Jnaar to anyone out of fear they might not believe him since he himself had doubts it actually happened.

Hunter opened his mouth to say something when Raaskar came to join them. The Jnaar looked grim, and Cameron wondered about the reason.

"Another runner just returned," Raaskar said.

"What did he say?" Hunter asked, not sounding overly enthusiastic, obviously expecting another negative report.

"He says he found the city where your female has been."

"Has been?" Hunter stared at the alien man. "Are you saying she was there but isn't there anymore? Is she dead?"

"Nobody knows. The warriors who saved her from a group of Dal Losos outside said she was in good spirits when she was brought to their city. But soon after, a mob of Shadow-dwellers came to invade their city. They took her, along with a number of other young females. That's all they know."

"Damn!" Hunter swore. "We're too late."

"Don't they know where she would have been taken?" Cameron prompted.

"We know of two large caverns inhabited by Shadow-dwellers. She may be in one of them." Raaskar hesitated. "If she is still alive."

"What is he saying," Malone asked. "Does he have news about the woman?"

"He has, but wherever she was, she isn't there anymore. Apparently, she's been abducted by the Shadow-dwellers. That's all he knows," Cameron told him.

"At least we have a trail we could follow." Malone sounded hopeful.

"And we will," Cameron assured him. "We need more information, though." He addressed Raaskar, "We would like to go to those caverns. Is it possible to get one of your people to guide us there?"

"We usually avoid going near the places where the Shadow-dwellers live, but I can find out if anyone is willing to accompany you."

"How far are the caverns you're talking about?"

Raaskar looked at Hunter. "The nearest is ten sleeping cycles away. The other one maybe fourteen. It depends how many obstacles come your way."

"What kind of obstacles?"

Raaskar made a clucking sound with his tongue. "You could be attacked by a band of Dal Losos, a group of Sras warriors may challenge your presence, or the tunnel may be blocked by a swarm of rock-crawlers."

"Rock-crawlers?"

"Don't let the name fool you. They are agile and can move swiftly on their eight legs. Small but ferocious with tiny, sharp teeth filling their mouths, they can inflict serious damage if they feel threatened. Luckily, they are not aggressive, only a nuisance to travelers. They shun bright lights and are easily discouraged from staying on their intended route." He chuckled. "They also provide a traveler with an excellent and tasty meal."

"We're prepared to deal with anything and anyone," Hunter said. "Our weapons are superior to the weapons the Sras and the Jnaar possess should any of the groups we meet decide to become hostile."

"You won't have to worry about hostile Jnaar if you are accompanied by one of our warriors. We don't fight each other. The Sras are a different story."

"I speak their language, remember?"

"So you've told me. They may not listen to reason. The Sras are violent and warlike."

"Then we will have to deal with them." Hunter gave a small sigh; his smile was thin and ferocious. "We humans are not exactly a peaceful race. Our history is full of violence and conflict. When we are attacked, we fight back."

Raaskar's purple eyes glinted. "Not much of our history has survived, but from what little we know, and from the legends our elders tell us, the history of the Jnaar is probably just as violent. We have not become weak. We also fight when attacked." His smile matched Hunter's. "We may not have the destructive weapons you humans possess, but we are quite proficient with the ones we have."

"I've seen you in action," Hunter agreed. "Even your mate is not afraid to fight."

Raaskar's expression softened. He chuckled. "That was nothing. You should see her when she gets angry with me. She is like an enraged Keeras. Don't tell her I said that. She may kill me in my sleep."

Hunter and Cameron laughed at his little joke. Malone looked from one to the other. "What did he say that was so funny? Damn, I wish I could understand him."

"He said his mate is a passionate woman," Hunter said, still chuckling.

"And that's funny?" Malone shook his head. "I think it's time we move on. And fast."

"You won't get any arguments from me," Cameron said. "Raaskar said it would take at least ten days to get to one of the caverns. Then we need a few days to find out if Regina is there. Should we be unsuccessful with our search, it'll take us ten days again to come back here. That's a minimum of at least twenty-four days. That is if things go well and we don't bump into any obstacles."

"A long time," Hunter agreed. "And then longer yet to check out the second cavern."

"That adds up to nearly two months," Cameron said. "Should we find her, hopefully alive, it will be time well worth spent, but what if she isn't in any of them? Then we'll have to search places even farther away."

"We could cut the time in half," Hunter mused.

"How?"

"By splitting up. You and Malone go to one cavern, while I go to the other one."

"Alone?"

"No. I wouldn't take that chance. Too dangerous, for one thing, and I don't feel like getting lost in these tunnels." He grinned. "Besides, if something should happen to me, who would record for the history books the heroic way I died?"

"None of us will die in these tunnels," Malone growled, giving Hunter an annoyed stare and then shifted his gaze to Cameron. "I think Hunter's plan has merits."

Cameron nodded slowly. "I don't like the idea of splitting up the team, but I have to agree. We'd save valuable time."

"I'm not exactly crazy about the idea, either," Hunter said grimly, but from his expression it was obvious to Cameron that he had made up his mind. "I'm the team leader and I've decided."

Cameron knew he wouldn't be able to talk Hunter out of it. "Then it's settled. We should get going as soon as possible."

"I'm ready to move." Malone sounded hopeful. "The sooner we start, the sooner we'll be on our way home."

Hunter chuckled. "You mean back to prison?"

Cameron threw a thoughtful look at the black man. "You like it here, don't you?"

"I could get used to living with these people." Hunter let his gaze roam across the sparkling ceiling and the alien, yet already familiar fauna surrounding them. "Life is simpler here and not bad. Better than being stuck inside that cozy giant egg Malone calls home for months at a time. I don't see that as my future."

"I have to agree with you," Cameron said, "but once the winter is over, you'll be able to leave the Station. How can you trade in the far-ranging spaces of the savannah teeming with wildlife and an open sky above you for this enclosed world where you can touch the ceiling if you had a long enough pole? Living in constant daylight, never be able to tell if it's day or night, not to experience different seasons? It would drive me crazy."

"The Jnaar don't stay underground all the time," Hunter argued. "As soon as the winter is over they go outside to hunt and get other supplies they can't get in here. The winter is only ten months long."

"Only ten months." Malone's rumbling laughter made Raaskar look at Hunter and Cameron.

"Your friend sounds like a lonely Ikkara looking for a female," Raaskar said with a chuckle.

Hunter grinned. "He's no Ikkara, but a night with a passionate female might calm him down."

"I may be able to arrange that," Raaskar said.

"Perhaps when we come back he'll be even more inclined and eager to accept your offer." Hunter became serious. "We'd like to start the search for our missing female as soon as we possibly can. We've talked it over and decided to split our team because of the time involved. I will be going to one of the caverns by myself. If you can find one warrior for me and one for Cameron and Malone who will go to the other location we'd be grateful."

"I will talk to Ruuro. He may know of someone." Before Raaskar left, he gave Cameron a wistful look. "You are beginning to master our language quite well, Cameron."

"I am getting better at it every day," Cameron said, pleased the Jnaar took notice. "But there are still many words and phrases I need to learn."

———

As it turned out, Ruuro had a twin brother who offered to guide Hunter. His name was Ramuuro. Ruuro also knew of a couple of warriors who were more than willing to go with Cameron and Malone. They were on their way four days after the decision to split was made.

One of the two warriors, Stasra, was the runner who had brought the news about Regina's whereabouts. He was tall and wiry, with long, muscular legs. Markas, the other guide, was shorter but stout and wide-shouldered.

According to Cameron's time-piece, it was early morning when the four men headed for one of the tunnels that led out of the cavern. Even after two months, he couldn't get used to the constant daylight, and it was almost a relief to enter the twilight of the tunnel.

Just before they walked deeper into the tunnel, someone called Cameron's name. He turned to see a figure hurrying toward them, carrying a spear in one hand. It was easy to see it was a female, and when she came closer Cameron recognized Carini, the mystery girl.

They waited for her, and Cameron wondered what she wanted.

"Rob," she said when she caught up with them. "I'm glad I got here in time."

"I've been looking for you everywhere, Carini," he said. "I was hoping to see you again."

She gave him an enigmatic smile. "I know."

"Why are you here?"

"I'm coming with you."

"Why?"

"So I can protect you." She pushed the point of her spear into the ground.

Cameron looked at the spear. "I have a feeling it will be my responsibility to protect you." He slapped his rifle with his free hand. "A spear is no match for my weapon."

"That may be so, but I know the tunnels, and I know the dangers. You don't."

"That's true, but I already have two guides." Cameron looked at the two warriors. "She wants to come with us."

Markas shrugged his massive shoulders. "That is her choice. If you accept her, we have no objections."

Cameron nodded, hoping he wouldn't regret his decision. "Okay."

She carried a pack made from leather on her back. Strapped to her waist, she had a skin filled with water and a leather sheath holding a knife. He realized she was well prepared and wouldn't have taken no for an answer, but he was puzzled, wondering about her real reason for coming along.

"Do you know this girl?" It was Malone who wanted to know.

"I met her some time ago," Cameron explained.

"You've never mentioned her."

"It was only a brief encounter and I forgot about her." Cameron didn't see any purpose in telling Malone about his involvement with her, as brief as it was.

"Why is she coming with us?"

"I don't know. She must have her reasons."

"Very strange," Malone said, shaking his head. "Why would a woman you barely know want to join our search? It doesn't make any sense. Do you trust her?"

Cameron grunted, annoyed at Malone for insisting on finding out more about Carini, especially since he was thinking along the same lines as Malone. "Like you said, I barely know her."

"I hope she won't become a problem."

The first day went by without any major obstacles. They spent the night in a small cavern. There were no shrubs or trees. Neither was there a pond in which to bathe, but a narrow river provided them with fresh water and a chance to wash. The ceiling of the cavern was not covered with the radioactive crystals to create daylight conditions. A few glow-roots clung to the ceiling and the walls, providing them with barely enough light, but it was sufficient. Cameron didn't mind. He had his headlamp should he be in need of more light.

He set up his Guard-Dog, which would warn them if unwanted visitors should drop by, but as it turned out it wasn't necessary. Cameron slept well, considering a thin blanket was the only cushion between his body and the hard surface of the tunnel floor. Fortunately, it was warm in the tunnels and they didn't need blankets to protect their bodies against cold drafts.

In the morning, Cameron and Malone ate from the rations they brought with them, not caring much for the strips of dried meat and vegetables the Jnaar offered them.

"I don't think I could ever get used to this," Malone grumbled as they moved on.

"Used to what?"

"The constant light in the caverns or the forever near darkness in the tunnels. Your system must get completely screwed up, not knowing if it's day or night. This is daytime, isn't it?"

Cameron looked at his wrist. "According to my computer, it's seven in the morning."

"The way my body feels it could be the middle of the night. I didn't sleep well. At times, I had the feeling I was lying on a bed of pointy, sharp rocks."

"I have no doubts you were." Cameron laughed. "Perhaps you're getting soft, Malone."

"You're probably right. I haven't seen any real action for a long time. A man needs to be active. It is the only way to live. I don't want to get used to the quiet, comfortable life."

"Some people don't mind the comfortable life. It is much safer. Men like you usually don't live very long."

"It's better to have lived a short but exciting life instead of a soft and boring long one." Malone shifted his laser rifle from one shoulder to another. "What good is a superior weapon if you can't use it once in a while?"

"Spoken like a true mercenary." Cameron threw a sidelong glance at the big man. "Why did you join the colonization program in the first place? You must have known there wouldn't be much demand for a mercenary."

"I can't give you an answer for that. Perhaps I thought planets a few hundred light-years from Earth would be different and more exciting. Maybe I was secretly hoping to discover a warlike alien race and my services as a soldier would be needed." His gaze rested on the two Jnaar warriors walking in front of him. "We've met members of an alien race, but they proved to be a disappointment."

"Their ancestors were probably superior to us when it came to technol-

23

ogy. In fact, these are only descendants of stranded alien space travelers. Their people are still out there somewhere. Perhaps we'll meet them someday. I hope they are peace loving, and our meeting with them will be peaceful."

"You sound like a typical civilian who loves the soft, boring life." Malone laughed.

"It does not have to be boring or soft, but I prefer to live a peaceful existence. There is nothing to be gained in warfare but misery and heartaches. People, and by that I include any alien race we may encounter, should be able to live together in harmony. Trading merchandise or knowledge instead of firing at each other with deadly weapons has always been more lucrative in the end for everyone involved." Cameron knew his words did not exactly resonate with Malone's beliefs. Malone was a mercenary, a soldier for hire. His life had always been hard and full of danger. Peace was not at the top of his list.

"You're an idealist, a dreamer." Malone spoke in an almost patronizing tone. "This universe is not peaceful, Cameron. It is violent and without mercy. Only through conflict does anything or anyone evolve and move forward. Peace brings about complacency. People get lazy and things turn stale. Most inventions happened because of necessity. When our primitive ancestors on Earth were confronted or hunted by the fierce predators roaming the primeval forests and savannahs, they developed weapons to defend themselves against those larger and stronger beasts. They used the same weapons against strangers who invaded their territory."

"I can't argue that," Cameron said, "but as people evolve and become more civilized you'd think their brains also evolve and they get more intelligent. They should realize that quarreling is not smart, but living in peace is. Individuals have a much better chance of reaching old age if they live together in harmony instead of fighting each other."

"It seems so logical, doesn't it, but unfortunately that's not the way it turned out. We humans can't suppress that killer gene we've inherited from our ancestors, no matter how hard we try. Sure, we think we are cultured and enlightened, but the thin veneer that separates us from animals, peels away quickly when we're confronted by hostile strangers. Our survival instincts kick in and we revert to what we really are…killer apes."

Cameron chuckled.

"What?" Malone spoke almost harshly.

"I didn't know you are such a philosopher, Malone, but I can't disagree with your deep thoughts," Cameron admitted grudgingly, acknowledging the big man made some sense. Any student of mankind's history could not deny the fact that humans were not a peaceful race. He chuckled again. "Who would have known you're not just a mountain of muscles but also a man with a brain."

"Well, thanks for the compliment." The sarcasm in Malone's words was obvious.

They walked on in silence for the remainder of the day, making only occasional comments about minor things. Their Jnaar guides spoke very little. They walked with an easy gait, appearing relaxed, but Cameron saw how their eyes scanned the darkness ahead of them and the way they held their spears. He knew they were alert and ready for any potential threats.

They spent the next resting period inside a small cave, barely large enough to provide room for them. Cameron woke up with stiff limbs. After eating some rations, they moved on. Nobody talked much. They only spoke to each other to make small comments.

Carini was oddly silent too. She barely paid any attention to Cameron, which he found somewhat disturbing and puzzling. Her last words to him by the pond that day echoed inside his head.

"I gave my body to you out of free will and you gave your body to me. From now on there is a bond between us. Next time we meet we won't be strangers anymore but friends, Rob Cameron."

What happened to that promise? A complete stranger couldn't be more distant than the way she acted.

Both and he and Malone walked with their headlamps switched on to illuminate the pebble-covered floor. Neither of them felt like stumbling over one of the many large rocks and getting injured. The Jnaar walked as surefooted as if it were daylight in the tunnel. He remembered Raaskar telling him that his species was able to see a broader spectrum with their large eyes than the humans.

Carini walked ahead of him, and he admired the shape of her lithe body and the sensuous way her full buttocks moved inside her short leather kilt. He had held those lovely globes of flesh, felt them quiver in his hands as she milked his engorged member. Thinking about their passionate and wild lovemaking by the pond caused his loins to flutter, and he felt like crushing her body against his, kissing her soft lips, and...

He stopped his thoughts from going in that direction, but the swaying of her hips in front of him made it nearly an impossible task.

As if sensing his thoughts, she suddenly slowed her walk and waited for him to catch up with her. Walking beside him, she glanced at him sideways. "Are you angry with me for joining you on your journey, Rob?" she asked.

Surprised by her question, he said, "No, I am not angry, only puzzled."

"Puzzled why?"

"Your reason. How did you know I was even going on this... this journey?"

She laughed softly. "It is no secret why you are here. Everyone knew about your plan."

"But how did you know when I would be leaving?"

"That also was no secret and easy to find out."

"How?"

"You were looking for warriors to guide you through the tunnels."

"That's true, but you're not a warrior. Why come along?"

"Just because I'm not a male doesn't mean I can't use a spear. I'm not a helpless female. You don't know anything about me, Rob."

Her somewhat sharp answer surprised him. "No, I don't." He gave her a lopsided grin. "I find you quite attractive when you get angry."

"I'm not angry."

"Well, I'm relieved to hear that. Since neither of us is angry, where do we go from here?"

"We follow the tunnel until we get to our destination, that's where." She laughed and fell back. "I'll be guarding your backs for a while. Sometimes predators like to attack from behind."

Malone, who had obviously been listening to his conversation with Carini, closed the gap between them. "What's the story with you and that girl, Cameron?"

"There is no story."

The big man let out a rumbling laugh. "I'm not exactly a dimwit, my friend. Even to a blind man it is obvious that your relationship with this girl goes deeper than just a casual meeting." He turned his head to look at Cameron. "Did you fuck her?"

Cameron snorted. "If I did it wouldn't be any of your business, Malone."

"No, it wouldn't be, but I'd be disappointed in you. There's a beautiful young woman waiting for you to come back to her. How'd you like it if she screwed another guy while you're gone?"

"You know the answer to that. No man likes to discover his woman screwed another guy."

"Then I don't have to guess how Valissa would react if she found out you had sexual relations with one of these Jnaar females." Malone threw a glance backwards at Carini. "To be honest, I can't blame you for having the hots for this one. She must be a hellcat in the sack." He laughed and rubbed his crotch.

Cameron was grateful knowing Carini didn't understand any of what Malone said, but she must be wondering what the two humans were discussing after seeing Malone checking her out. No woman misses a thing like that.

"I never said I had sexual relations with her, but think what you will, Malone. Just don't make a big deal out of it. Perhaps now we can drop the subject?"

"No problem."

Malone moved his head in a semicircle and played the light from his headlamp across the rough stones. Cameron thought he detected something disappearing into one of the holes in the ceiling, but when he shone his light on the spot, he didn't see anything.

The two guides stopped walking and peered into the shadowy gloom ahead of them. They stood silent and seemed to listen intently. Markas closed his eyes for a quick moment and sniffed the air.

"Problems?" Cameron spoke with a subdued voice, trying to penetrate the darkness with his eyes. The light from his lamp didn't reveal anything but a few small boulders scattered across the tunnel floor. Anything could hide behind those boulders.

"There may be trouble ahead," Markas said.

"What kind of trouble?"

The guide shrugged his wide shoulders. "I smell Dal Losos."

"Dal Losos?" Cameron repeated. "Are they dangerous?"

"You know what they are?"

"Not really."

27

"When the Shadow-dwellers mate with the daughters of the Dark Goddess they produce offspring that are neither Jnaar nor spawn of the Dark Goddess. They are different. The males are handsome and the females beautiful. They don't seem to age, but they do. When they reach a certain age, their bodies begin to rot and change. Instead of eating vegetable matter they crave meat." Markas grimaced. "I believe you will meet the Dal Losos shortly."

"Can they be killed?"

Markas chuckled. "They are already dead, but their bodies can be destroyed. Not easily, but it is possible."

Cameron lifted his laser rifle. "This will kill them."

"Maybe." The expression on the alien's face revealed his doubts.

Cameron couldn't blame him. Markas had never witnessed the destructive power the lasers could unleash. The energy bolt from a laser turned rock, even metal, into lumps of lava. Rotten flesh and brittle bones would leave few traces after being hit with a spray of scorching heat. He was confident these Dal Losos would pose no great danger.

Slowly, they walked forward, eyes darting from left to right, alert for any sudden movement. It came as a surprise when dark forms suddenly appeared out of a tunnel hidden behind an outcropping of rock. The creatures moved in eerie silence as they shambled toward them.

Naked, their filthy emaciated bodies were full of open sores. Some looked like walking skeletons. Cameron could scarcely believe they were still alive. When he looked into their faces, he saw frozen masks of rotting flesh and dead eyes in sunken sockets.

Dal Losos.

Cameron didn't have much time to contemplate the horrors in front of him when he heard Malone cursing beside him. A flash from Malone's weapon sliced one of the creatures neatly in half. The lower body shuffled on for a few steps after the upper torso toppled to the ground, skeletal fingers scratching the hard surface of the tunnel floor. None of his companions seemed to notice his demise. They stumbled over his fallen body, arms flailing, and mouths wide open, displaying rotten teeth.

With a silent curse, Cameron aimed his weapon at the nearest of the Dal Losos and squeezed the trigger, releasing a series of white energy bolts. The emaciated body collapsed into a lifeless heap of scorched bones and flesh.

Before he could target another of the creatures, the two guides and Carini reached the shambling band of near-beasts and attacked them with their spears, dispatching three of the nearest with well-aimed thrusts into their narrow chests. Cameron watched as one of the remaining four tried to sink its claws into Carini's naked arm. Taking aim, Cameron sliced off the creature's arm at the shoulder.

Moving his laser a fraction, he burned another one. Malone took care of a second. There was only one left, and Stasra rammed his spear into its belly, causing entrails to spill like giant worms crawling out of their den. Then he used his knife to chop off the skull-like head. It rolled across the rocky floor, its jaw moving until if finally lay still.

Cameron flashed his light past the small mountain of dead bodies, searching for more of them, but the tunnel was empty. He smelled a terrible stench and tried to take shallow breaths. It would be good to get away from this spot as quickly as possible, but he was afraid the stench would stay with him for a while.

Stasra turned to look at the humans. A smile lit his handsome face. "As you see, they can be destroyed." He became serious. "Those are terrible weapons," he said, his chin pointing in the direction of Cameron's rifle.

"They are," Cameron agreed. "In the wrong hands, they could spell disaster."

Stasra nodded thoughtfully. "Yes, they could, but I wish I could possess at least one such weapon. It would be enough to slaughter our enemies."

"If you mean the Sras then I'm glad you don't have any of these weapons," Cameron growled. "I was told some of our people have friends among the Sras. Hunter has."

"The Sras are our sworn enemies," Stasra said vehemently. "We will never be friends with them. Never! Our people have been feuding as long as we can remember."

"Perhaps if the Sras and the Jnaar would change their attitude toward each other you might just end this feud. It would be good for both races."

"That will never happen." Stasra looked into the darkness ahead. "We should move forward."

# CHAPTER THREE

NOT MUCH HAPPENED FOR THE NEXT FOUR DAYS. ON THE EVENING OF THE eighth day they walked into a small, brightly lit cavern. Not far from the entrance they found a pond fed by a trickle of fresh water coming out of a crack in the rock wall.

Before any of them ventured farther into this apparent idyllic paradise, the three Jnaar searched the ceiling and the walls for any signs of danger.

"Watch the shrubs and trees," Markas cautioned. "Anything can hide inside or behind them."

Cameron used his wrist gadget to scan the cavern for indications of larger life forms but didn't detect anything. Nothing but flickers of smaller energy emanations. It didn't mean there was no danger in the cavern. Even small animals could pose a threat if they were vicious and possibly poisonous.

"I think we can relax. At least for now," he said to Malone, who was watching him anxiously.

"It is safe," Markas declared, confirming Cameron's findings.

"I will wash," Carini announced, and began disrobing. "Anyone want to join me?" she said, glancing at Cameron. Naked, she walked to the edge of the pond and slid into the water.

Cameron watched her, surprised by her unabashed behavior. The sight of her voluptuous naked body, the movement of her plump buttocks, the swing of her hips, made him remember their passionate sexual encounter by the pond in the Jnaar city.

"She certainly isn't shy," Malone remarked with a sidelong glance at Cameron. "How did you say you two met?"

"I never told you." Cameron had no intentions telling Malone anything.

The two guards didn't seem bothered by Carini's nakedness. In fact, after putting their weapons and packs onto the ground, they took off their clothes and jumped into the water.

"Go ahead and join them, Cameron," Malone said. "I'll stand guard until you're finished. I'd feel uneasy about all of us being in the water and our weapons back on land. One never knows what or who can suddenly come for a little visit." He grinned. "I don't want to be caught with my pants down."

Shrugging off his pack, Cameron let it slide to the grass-covered ground. Then he laid his laser on top of his pack and undressed. "Good idea. I'll follow your advice. I feel sweaty and grimy."

Looking around one more time to make certain there were no unwanted guests watching, he walked to the pond and stepped into the water. It was cool but not cold. With a satisfied sigh, he sank down and ducked his head under the surface, enjoying the refreshing sensation on his naked skin. The clear water revealed Carini's lower body nearby. She was facing in his direction. Her image was somewhat blurry but distinct enough to see the slit in the puffy mound of her sex-organ, triggering pangs of desire in his body and mind.

He surfaced and swam away from her toward the other side of the pond. Finding a spot behind a short tongue of land stretching into the pond and out of view from the others, he tried to sort out his thoughts. His mind was in turmoil and sudden guilt wracked him. How could he desire another woman when Valissa was waiting faithfully back at the Station? She was the only woman he loved. She trusted him, and he had broken her trust already. It was done. There was nothing he could do about it, but he could prevent it from happening again.

Damn it! He wasn't some kind of animal in heat who had to screw every woman who was willing to let him. He heard splashing sounds behind him and turned around to see Carini swimming toward him with powerful strokes. She smiled and rose up in front of him, close enough to rub her small breasts against his chest.

"Are you trying to avoid me?" Her hand snaked down his belly and touched his penis.

"Don't," he gasped. The touch of her hand was like an electric shock.

She laughed and put her other hand behind his head, pulling him close. Her lips felt hot on his. He pushed her away, almost violently.

Pouting, she stared at him. Her large, alien eyes studied his face. "What is wrong?"

"Everything," he replied hoarsely. "This is not right. Besides, we are not alone."

"They can't see us here. Even if they could, they wouldn't care."

"I care."

"Why?"

"I have a woman waiting for me to come back to her. I've been unfaithful already once. It won't happen again." He spoke with a rough voice, trying to convince himself.

"You told me about your mate before, and I told you she is not here. She will never know about us, unless you tell her." She swam closer. Laying one hand on his chest, she gave him an alluring smile. "Your secret is safe with me. Besides, I don't understand why joining with me is being unfaithful. Among the Jnaar a male and a female will join their bodies without reservation." She put a finger on his lips. "The first time we met you seemed different. You found delight in my arms as I did in yours. When we parted I told you there is a special bond between us. There still is, more than you know."

Her eyes seemed to glow softly as she spoke. He felt a quiet pulling in his head. When she touched his penis again, it grew hard inside her hand. With a moan, he pulled her close and kissed her. Laughing into his mouth, she let go of him and grabbed his hand. He followed her as she pulled him toward land, his desire for her a burning flame between his legs.

She climbed on land and lay on her back, her legs wide open. Her purple eyes drew him to her the way a bright light attracts a creature of the night accustomed only to the dark. Her lips formed a smile.

"Come," she whispered. Her arms beckoned.

His gaze fastened on the hairless bulge of her sex-organ, and then on the narrow pink slit that seemed to pulse with a life of its own. This felt right. He was doing nothing wrong. He fell between her spread legs. His rigid organ stabbed frantically, searching for a way to still the sudden hunger, to soothe the terrible ache.

Sliding into her warm, moist canal, he shouted with joy as the soft walls closed with gentle pressure around his throbbing member. Moving frantically in and out of her, he was oblivious of his surroundings. The only thing that mattered was the unbelievable joy he experienced in Carini's embrace. She wrapped her strong legs around his buttocks; her lower body gyrated beneath him with vigor as she milked his hard penis.

Sobbing, he exploded inside her, filling her vessel with his gift. When he came down from his euphoria after what seemed like an eternity, he lay in her arms, gasping for breath. Her hands stroked his back gently; her mouth made soothing sounds.

"What happened?" he stammered, his breath still coming in great gasps.

She laughed softly and held him tight. "You don't remember?"

He lifted his head and stared into her alien eyes. "You seduced me," he said with an accusing tone.

"Didn't you enjoy our joining?"

"You know I did. I feel like an animal in heat, unable to control my urges. How did you do it? What did you do?"

"I didn't have to do anything. Your hormones reacted with my emanations. You couldn't help it. You've been conditioned by someone in the past."

"Conditioned? I don't know what you're talking about."

"What was her name?"

"Her name is Valissa."

"Your mate?"

"Yes."

She relaxed her legs and freed him from her embrace. He was still stiff when he pulled out of her. His desire for her was strong, but he fought it.

"Not your mate," she said. "There was someone else."

How could she know? What was it about this alien woman that mesmerized him?

"Tell me about her," Carini said softly.

"She called herself Xandra." He spoke slowly as if having trouble remembering, but that wasn't true. The memory of the alien entity was strong in his mind. It would never leave him. "She was not human. Neither was she Jnaar. She was something else entirely.

She called herself a goddess." He paused. "Perhaps she was. She possessed great powers."

"She did something to your mind." It was not a question but a statement.

"I don't know what she did." He rolled onto his back and stared at the sparkling ceiling of the cavern. Oh, but he knew.

*I put a tiny piece of myself into you so I could see what you see and hear what you hear.* She had told him so herself. Part of the Xandra was in his skull. After she repaired the injuries to his body, she put a biological transmitter into him to use him as a spy.

What else did she do? He had left her influence. There were millions of kilometers between him and her, but she was still with him. Was it possible that whatever the Xandra did to him could be used against him here on the fifth planet?

Carini turned onto her side and looked at him. He was struck again by the eerie likeness of the Jnaar females and the Xandra. The first time he met the Xandra her eyes had been like the eyes of the Jnaar.

"You are so beautiful," he heard himself saying.

It was the truth. Her large eyes and long lashes emphasized the delicate beauty of her face. Her body was perfect, almost too perfect, an artist's dream. Yet Carini was no exception. All the Jnaar females were beautiful.

Her silvery laugh enchanted and put him under her spell. Shaking her long hair out of her eyes, she bent over him and put her soft lips on his. She tasted sweet and intoxicating. He put his arms around her slim body and pulled her on top of him. His stiff pole slid easily back into her creamy sheath. She rotated her pelvis slowly, while her inner walls pulsed gently around his throbbing member.

Delirious from the pleasure she gave him, he forgot about Valissa, forgot where he was. Her eyes were locked with his. He saw nothing else, only her eyes. They seemed to look deep into his soul, seemed to read his inner thoughts.

"Let it happen," she whispered softly. "Relax and let it happen."

His mind swam in a black void filled only with pleasure. It was easy to let go and immerse himself in this void, easy to meld his mind with...

*Welcome to my world, Rob Cameron.*

The ghostly voice sounded loud and clear. He wanted to open his eyes but couldn't. An alien presence took over his body and kept it immobile. A vision formed in front of his mind's eye. He saw a woman, dressed in flowing robes, with long hair that moved like a nest of snakes. She looked familiar and yet different.

*Xandra?*

He wanted to scream it aloud but his vocal cords refused to obey.

Silent laughter seemed to mock him. *I am not she.*

A terrible truth dawned on him. *You are the one they call the Dark Goddess.*

*Yes, I am.*

*How do you know my name?*

*I read it in your mind. I've been aware of you ever since you entered this underground world. Your mind is different from the others. I am curious about you.*

The vision and the alien presence were gone in an instant. When he opened his eyes, he looked into the purple eyes of Carini. She smiled enigmatically.

"She is waiting for you." Before he could open his mouth, she offered him her breast. Without thinking, he fastened his lips on the thick nipple and sucked on it. Sweet, familiar tasting liquid flowed into his mouth, giving him instant stamina.

"Who are you?" he asked with a strangled voice.

She laughed gently. "I am Carini."

"No. Carini's breasts did not taste like this." He heaved up against her, moaned when incredible pleasure washed through his body.

"They didn't because I controlled the flow of my nectar."

"You are one of her creatures," he said, shuddering as a climax rocked his body.

"It is true. She made me, but I am not one of her creatures. I am her daughter. There is a difference."

He was barely aware of her words. He gave in to the pleasure that radiated from his groin as it spread through his system. His penis jumped inside her milking pussy. When the pleasure subsided, sanity returned for a moment and her words became clear.

"Are you telling me you can hide your true identity?"

She nodded.

"You told me you had a brother. Is he like you?"

Nodding again, she gave a little chuckle. "There are many of us among the Jnaar. They suspect, but they don't know."

She kissed him and dribbled sweet saliva into his mouth. He swallowed eagerly. Then he turned with her until she was on her back. Moving with renewed vigor between her spread thighs, he pushed all caution deep into his subconscious. She kept him in her embrace and let him ride her until he nearly dropped from exhaustion.

They fell asleep in each other's arms. He didn't care if the others found them like that or not.

———

CARINI WAS GONE when he awoke. Sitting up, he looked around and groaned when memory flooded his consciousness.

The Xandra! She was here.

No, not the Xandra, but another entity like her.

The Dark Goddess. She was like the Xandra, and she was aware of him. How could that be? Perhaps it had all been a bad dream. He remembered having sex with Carini. For hours, at least that what he seemed to remember. He should feel exhausted, even after a long sleep, but he felt rested, invigorated even.

Looking down at himself he realized he was naked. His clothes were on the other side of the pond.

Where was Carini?

He heard the sounds of someone approaching. Looking up, he recognized Malone. The big man stepped around a clump of thick shrubs. When he saw Cameron, he shook his head.

"This is where you're hiding. When I saw you and that female disappear I somehow knew I wouldn't be seeing you for a while, but you spent the whole night here, away from our little camp. Very careless."

Cameron gave him a sheepish look. "I wasn't really alone."

"But for how long? When I went to sleep you two weren't there, but when I woke up, and that was hours ago, I saw the female sleeping beside our guides. For some reason, I assumed you were also nearby, but this morning I discovered I was wrong." Malone seemed suddenly angry. "I can't condone what you're doing. You may be putting all of us in danger. We need to stay together."

"Did you say Carini is in the camp?" Cameron didn't know what else to say. He knew Malone was right.

"I saw her before down by the pond washing up."

Cameron wiped his brow. "Something strange happened to me last night," he said, wondering if he should tell Malone about Carini and his contact with the Dark Goddess.

Malone snorted like an angry stallion. "I don't need to hear any explicit details, Cameron. You two made enough noise to leave no doubt as to what you were doing. I guess you don't really care much about that sweet girl you left behind, the one who's counting on you coming back safe and sound. The one who trusts you to be faithful to her."

"You know nothing about me and how I feel, Malone," Cameron said angrily. "There is much more at stake here than you can ever imagine. Carini is not what she seems."

"Are you saying she's not female?" Malone let out a sarcastic laugh. "She looks female to me."

"Don't be stupid, Malone. Of course she's a female. What I mean, she is not a Jnaar. She's a creature of the Dark Goddess."

When he looked into Malone's face, he saw nothing but pity, but also an expression of great concern. "Are you feeling all right, Cameron? Perhaps you should tell me about the strange thing that happened to you last night."

Cameron made the decision to tell Malone about the Dark Goddess after all but struggled to find the right words. As he was about to talk Carini came into view. She smiled at Cameron.

"I hope you're not angry I left you, but you were sleeping so deeply, I didn't want to disturb your sleep."

"I'm not angry," he told her. "Just confused."

She handed him a bundle she'd been carrying. "I brought your clothes." She gave him an innocent, almost shy look. "I hope you feel rested. I feel a bit sore. You seemed insatiable."

Cameron threw a quick glance at Malone, glad the big man didn't understand what he and Carini were discussing. "The only reason I was insatiable was the fact that you made me suck on your breast and fed me your arousing nectar."

"You didn't enjoy sucking my breast?"

"Of course I did. You know what I'm talking about. Your breast, your saliva, all designed to give a male stamina and to keep him under your control."

"I don't know what you're talking about." She shook her head. "The only time my breasts will secrete any nectar is after my offspring has hatched from its egg so I can give it nourishment. My breasts are dry now."

"What about the Dark Goddess? You told me you're one of her daughters."

Carini stared at him. He couldn't read the expression on her face, but it was clear she wondered about his sanity the same way Malone had done.

"Why would I tell you something crazy like that? I am a Jnaar. Have you been inhaling ilia-spores?"

"What are ilia-spores?"

"They make you imagine things, see things that aren't real."

Cameron closed his eyes, wondering if he had suffered from an illusion. "Did you and I join our bodies after we swam in the pond or did I imagine that too?" He opened his eyes to look at her.

She chuckled. "You didn't imagine that." Then her face became serious. "You acted somewhat strangely. I wondered about the stamina you displayed. It seemed you didn't want to stop. Now it makes sense." She walked away from him and began examining the shrubs and trees surrounding them.

"What is she looking for?" Malone had been watching closely.

Cameron shrugged. "I'm not quite sure. She thinks I may have been exposed to some spores."

"It wouldn't surprise me. Suggesting this female is a daughter of the Dark Goddess is preposterous and sounds like the ravings of a madman. What were you going to tell me before she came?"

"It's not important now. My mind may have fabricated the whole thing. You're right, it sounds ridiculous and stupid."

He turned to look at Carini when he heard her exclaim loudly. "Here it is," she said triumphantly, holding a small, bright-red sac between her fingers. "Ilia-spores. There are enough in here to make all of us see and hear things that exist only in our imagination. They are dangerous." Her gaze rested on Cameron. "You must have inhaled some of these. That's why you acted so strangely. I should have known."

"What is she saying?" Malone asked. "And what's in that red bag she's holding?"

"Hallucinogenic spores. She thinks I've inhaled some of those."

Malone seemed to relax. "At least it explains a lot. Maybe you have an excuse after all for the way you've been behaving. Now, let's have breakfast and then we should be on our way." He looked at Carini and the sac of spores she was still displaying. "Tell her to put that away carefully before it bursts. I don't feel like bringing any of that stuff that is buried in my subconscious to life."

Before Cameron could relay Malone's request, Carini knelt down and dug a small hole with her fingers. She put the red sac into it and spread a little soil over the hole. She rose and walked toward the two men.

"There is no danger now."

"Good." He quickly dressed while Carini and Malone waited for him.

The two guides were sitting cross-legged, eating from their dry provisions. They didn't say anything, just nodded, throwing a brief glance at Cameron. Carini remained equally silent. She sat and opened her pack. Pulling out a few strips of dried meat, she put one into her mouth and chewed on it, looking in the direction of the pond.

Cameron picked up his backpack and removed one of the ration packs. Ripping it open with his teeth, he waited for it to expand and warm up. It was supposed to simulate bacon and eggs, but for some reason it didn't taste like much.

It appeared Malone felt the same way. "I'd give a lot right now to eat some real meat and drink a glass of fine wine," he complained.

Cameron grinned. "For breakfast?"

"It could easily be supper. How can you tell with this constant light in here and the twilight in the tunnels what time of day it is?"

"I can." Cameron lifted his left arm.

"Well, you're lucky to have a device like that. I don't have one," Malone growled.

The guides rose at the same time. The tall one, Stasra, came over to the two humans. "We should be moving," he said.

"We're ready," Cameron told him.

A short time later they were back in the tunnel.

It was late in the afternoon when Stasra stopped walking and waited for

Cameron to catch up with him. "We will spend the next rest period here, but this is as far as we accompany you. Tomorrow you must go on alone."

Cameron gave him a surprised look. "Why? I thought you would lead us right to the place where the Shadow-dwellers live?"

"We are close, but we do not dare to walk with you any farther. They would capture us and turn us into slaves."

"What about us?"

"You will become slaves... or even worse." He shrugged. "Unless you can kill them all with your magic weapons."

"That's not our intention," Cameron said, smiling grimly. "Before we kill anyone, we like to convince them that we come in peace."

Stasra's expression didn't change. "I wish you success with that."

There was not much protection anywhere, so they slept close to the wall. Cameron set up his Guard-Dog, which provided them with a measure of security, but he didn't sleep well that night.

He woke up sore from lying on the hard surface. Nobody said much during breakfast. When they were done, Cameron addressed Stasra. "I guess we can't persuade you to stay a little longer with us?"

The guard shook his head. "We cannot. From here on you are on your own."

"No, they are not," Carini said. "I will stay with them."

"Aren't you afraid of becoming a prisoner of the Shadow-dwellers?" Cameron said.

In a way, he had almost expected her to stay. The memory of what happened between them among the shrubs on the other side of the pond was still strong with him. He knew that had been real, but had he been hallucinating when she confessed she was a daughter of the Dark Goddess? He didn't know, but he might soon find out the truth. Her offer to stay made him suspicious again.

Her eyes met his. "I promised to protect you and I will not break my promise."

He had turned his headlamp so it would shine its light against the ceiling, but there was enough brightness to see her face clearly. Something in her expression kept him from making a remark about the things he seemed to remember her telling him during their passionate lovemaking. He forced a smile.

"I appreciate your offer, but I told you this when you joined us. Your spear cannot compete with my weapon. You've seen what it can do. You are not obligated to come with us as a protector."

"Then let me come as your guide. You don't know what you'll be facing."

"And you do?" He baited her on purpose, but she just shrugged.

"This is my world. I am familiar with it. You aren't. You'd be wise to take my offer."

Cameron looked at the two male Jnaar. "Will she be safe?"

Markas lifted one thick shoulder. "Probably not, but it is her choice." He chuckled sardonically. "She's got long legs. The Dal Losos move slowly. She'll easily outrun them."

"I won't run away from the Dal Losos," Carini said, visibly suppressing her sudden anger. "I'm a warrior like you and not afraid of anyone or anything."

Markas grinned. Then he punched Cameron on one arm. "She has fire in her body and she seems to have taken a liking to you." He winked. "Among the Jnaar it is bad luck if a male rejects a female. Accept her and what she offers you."

The two guides grabbed their gear and weapons and left. Cameron looked after them until they disappeared in the darkness of the tunnel.

Turning to Carini, he said, "In a way I'm glad you're staying, but I fear for your safety."

She smiled and touched his cheek in a gentle gesture. "Thank you for worrying, but there is no need. It is you who needs protection. You will soon understand. Now, I suggest we move on."

"Time to go," Cameron said to Malone.

Malone shrugged into his backpack. "Too bad our guides deserted us. I hope she knows where we're going."

"She says she does. According to the guides, we are close to our destination. We'll have to be careful. We don't want to come across as hostile intruders. Having Carini with us may be a good thing. She may be able to introduce us to the Shadow-dwellers."

It was shortly after noon when a group of armed warriors stepped into their path, spears ready to be thrown.

"Wait here," Carini told Cameron. Then she walked up to the first warrior.

Cameron couldn't hear what she was saying, but after a few tense moments the warriors lowered their spears and stepped back into the shadows. Carini turned around and waved for Cameron and Malone to come.

"You'll be safe." She smiled. "You've been expected."

# CHAPTER FOUR

HUNTER WOULD HAVE PREFERRED THE TEAM STAY TOGETHER, BUT HE KNEW to split up was the only practical way. They needed to cut the search time in half. He and Ramuuro were on their way the day after Cameron and Malone left.

They made good progress the first day. The smooth tunnel floor was well lit by glow-lichen. It was bright enough to see where they were going, and Hunter barely used his headlamp, especially since Ramuuro suggested it was better to walk without the bright light advertising their presence. They slept in a small cave cut into the tunnel wall. Ramuuro wanted to sleep in shifts, but Hunter assured him it wasn't necessary. He trusted Dawn, the AI strapped to his wrist, to warn him of potential dangers. Ramuuro wasn't quite convinced and insisted they partially block the narrow entrance to the cave with rocks, in addition to wedging his spear into a crevice, with its sharp point facing the entrance.

"The stones will alert us to anything and anyone trying to enter." Ramuuro smiled grimly. "And the spear will convince them of their fool-ishness."

"The spear won't stop a slithering serpent or any other small animal," Hunter argued.

"That is true, but my ears are trained to hear them as they move over the rocks. You seem to forget that this is my world, Hunter. My people have survived in these tunnels for a long time. We are familiar with all the sounds and smells."

Hunter touched the device on his wrist. "I may not know much about your world, but I've been to other, more hostile worlds, and I have learned to trust my gadgets. We'll be safe."

"Good, then let us get a good rest. Tomorrow may be more strenuous than today."

Hunter made himself comfortable on the hard ground. Not wanting to appear worried, he didn't ask Ramuuro what he meant with his remark about a strenuous day ahead, but he wondered. Other than that, he slept well. No hostile animals or people tried to disturb their sleep. He woke feeling rested.

The tunnel narrowed as they walked. At times, the ground became steep and more and more difficult to negotiate. To make it even more difficult, the rock under their feet was wet and slippery.

"This tunnel is hardly used," Ramuuro explained and chuckled. "We do not communicate much with the Shadow-dwellers."

"But they do come to your city sometimes, don't they?"

"Not from this direction. There are other tunnels which they use. We don't know all of them. There are many tunnels below and above us. Some of them are too dark and dangerous to travel safely while others are too narrow."

"Speaking of glow-lichen…" Hunter switched on his headlamp. It had been getting darker gradually as the glow-lichen on the ceiling slowly disappeared. A particularly narrow part ahead made him wonder if their journey would end here, but Ramuuro didn't seem to be worried.

He squeezed his bulky body through the narrow cleft. Hunter followed him slowly with misgivings, hoping it wouldn't be this difficult to move on for the rest of the way. They made it through the narrow part with little difficulty. Looking back, Hunter noticed that the tunnel walls had collapsed on this spot and, playing his light across the ceiling, he saw large cracks with rocks hanging precariously between them, threatening to fall and close the tunnel completely.

"We don't need your light anymore," Ramuuro told him after a while. "The glow-roots throw enough light for us to see."

The next few days passed without many obstacles blocking their way except for the occasional Larroth; small, lizard-like creatures that hissed loudly, displaying a double row of sharp teeth while putting on a show of bravado. They usually scuttled away with their tails pointed high as soon as the two travelers came too close. One time they encountered a Grala, one of those giant snakes with the huge, grotesque head. Hunter remembered the Grala from the time after entering the underground world when he almost had his head bitten off had it not been for Raaskar's quick reaction. Ignorance could be deadly, but he had learned to be more alert since then. Born and growing up on Emerald, a planet with a variety of dangerous wildlife, it didn't take him long to fall back into a life he had once led.

On the thirteenth day, their way was suddenly blocked by a party of warriors.

"Shadow-dwellers," Ramuuro hissed loud enough for Hunter to hear.

"I guessed as much," Hunter hissed back.

Even though they were Jnaar in appearance, something about them made him suspect their true nature. Their short kilts were adorned with the outline of a naked female stitched into the leather, and their heads were bald.

"You are trespassing," the leader of the group said harshly. "You are our prisoners. Resist and you will be killed."

Hunter lifted his free hand. "We are not seeking conflict with you. We came to talk to your queen."

"She is not our queen. She is a goddess," the speaker informed him. He studied Hunter with curiosity. "You are a stranger," he observed. "From the outside."

"Yes, I am. Have you seen people like me before? Possibly a female?"

The warrior didn't reply. He turned to the other warriors behind him. "Take them," he ordered.

Hunter and Ramuuro offered no resistance. The warriors took their backpacks from them, and Hunter's rifle. His first impulse was to refuse, but then he realized if he wanted to have any chance in finding Regina, he had to let himself be taken prisoner. Reluctantly, he handed over the weapon. They walked surrounded by their captors. "I am looking for a female of my kind," Hunter said. "Do you know anything about her?"

They didn't answer. He gave up after a few unsuccessful attempts, hoping he'd find out soon.

After about an hour's walk, they entered a brightly lit cavern, much larger and higher than the one the Jnaar occupied. At first, Hunter almost believed they had left the mountains and emerged on the outside, but he knew that wasn't possible because it was the middle of winter and a thick blanket of snow covered the ground. Lush green vegetation grew everywhere. Tall trees rose almost as high as the ceiling, and many of the shrubs were laden with fruit. The air smelled fresh with a strong hint of flowers, and he heard the twittering of birds and the humming of insects.

When he stopped to take it all in, he was pushed forward by one of the warriors and nearly stumbled over a root snaking across the path. His initial reaction was to strike out at the warrior, but he controlled his impulse. He needed to stay calm, which meant showing no aggression. The path ended suddenly, and he looked at a number of buildings similar to the one in the Jnaar city.

They stopped in front of a building that was taller and larger than the others. The door opened and as Hunter entered the darkened interior he wondered what waited for them inside.

Only two of the warriors accompanied him and Ramuuro through a second door. He found himself facing an assembly of men seated behind a long table and remembered the day when he and his group arrived at the Jnaar city.

The men appeared to be young, but when Hunter looked into their large, dark eyes, he saw great age and little pity. To these men he was nothing but a curiosity, someone or something to be studied, to be dissected, like an interesting bug or a weird plant.

All eyes were on him. They seemed to ignore Ramuuro. Nobody spoke. They just watched.

"We come in peace," Hunter finally said, the silence making him crawl inside. At every moment, he expected them to change into some hideous creatures with mouths full of teeth and tentacles for arms. He didn't know why he would think that.

One of them broke their silence. "Why are you here?" he asked. His voice was full and melodic but cold, with no empathy or any hint he and Ramuuro might be welcome.

"One of my people, a female, has been abducted and brought into your world. We have information she has been captured by Shadow-dwellers."

"And you think she is here?"

"I was hoping she would be."

"Why?"

"If she is still alive, I want to take her back with me to her people."

"She may not want to come back with you."

"That is her choice. Is she here?"

"I didn't say she was."

"But you know about her?"

The speaker didn't reply for a long moment. He just stared into emptiness, making Hunter wonder if he had gone to sleep or into some kind of trance. None of the others spoke, either. They sat inert and motionless, like statues. The only indication the men were alive and not some immobile, dead replicas of living entities, was the glittering of their cold black eyes.

Hunter waited impatiently for an answer. After a while he couldn't stand the silence any longer. "Who are you people anyway?"

"We are the Councilors of the Dark Goddess," one of them said.

"We are the Guardians," another one said.

"Where is this Dark Goddess?" Hunter asked boldly. "I'd like to meet her."

"Why?" one asked.

"I'm curious to find out if she really exists. I've heard so much about her."

They all smiled suddenly. "She exists. Be careful what you wish for. You may not like what you find."

"Or perhaps I will like what I find. How do you know?" He paused. "You haven't given me an answer about the woman I seek. Do you know anything about her?"

"Your question will be answered in good time. For now, consider yourself our guest. Be warned; do not wander around. This is not a place without dangers." The speaker waved a hand. "Now, go with the warriors. They will take you to your quarters."

Hunter and Ramuuro followed the two warriors outside and then down a narrow path. They passed a small pond partially hidden behind some shrubbery. Hunter caught a brief glimpse of people swimming in the water, but then he saw one of them quite clearly... a naked young woman.

*Things can't be too bad here. Not with nude women frolicking in the* water. Perhaps they'd get a chance to join them. That wouldn't be too dangerous. A little smile formed on his lips. Then again, it could be.

He expected to be taken to one of those huts, but was disappointed when their two guards stopped in front of a gate made from thick iron bars. The gate barred the entrance to a small cave.

"In there," one of the warriors told them.

"I thought we were guests?" Hunter protested.

"You are, but until we have established your true purpose here you'll be confined in here."

"What about our belongings?"

"They will be returned to you in good time."

"May we ask for some food and water?"

"It will be supplied."

Reluctantly, Hunter and Ramuuro entered the cave. After Hunter's eyes adjusted to the dim light inside, he saw a couple of woven carpets covering part of the stone floor in the back of the cave, with a few pillows piled up on one of them. He didn't have to ask what the clay pot in one corner was meant for. He turned when he heard the gate click into place behind him.

"This is a prison," he said to Ramuuro.

His companion grunted. "What did you expect? We're lucky they didn't kill us," he rumbled.

"Isn't that what you anticipated all along?" Hunter was surprised by Ramuuro's pessimistic attitude.

"I was hoping I would be wrong."

"Well, you were. They won't kill us. They're much too curious to find out more about us, especially me. By the way, did you see those girls in the pond?"

Ramuuro nodded.

"I didn't get to see much, but from what I saw they weren't some kind of monstrous creatures." He grinned. "The girl I saw was naked and looked pretty attractive to me."

"What about the Guardians of the Dark Goddess?" Ramuuro wondered. "Did you look into their eyes?"

Hunter shuddered, remembering. "So you noticed that, too?"

"What did you notice?"

"I saw age and wisdom, and cruelty," he mused. "But I also saw curiosity, and that's a good sign. Like I said, they won't kill us." He looked at the blan-kets, and then at his wrist-gadget to see what time it was. "I suggest we get some rest. I'm tired, actually."

Hunter woke to the rattling of the gate and sat up to see it swing open. A warrior stood in the doorway and threw their stuff onto the ground. Without looking at the prisoners, he locked the gate again and walked away. Rubbing the sleep from his eyes, Hunter noticed that Ramuuro was already sitting cross-legged on his blanket. It seemed he had been watching Hunter sleeping.

Rising to his feet, Hunter walked over to the entrance of their prison and picked up his backpack and rifle. "They promised us food and water," he said, his voice still thick from sleep. He rummaged in his pack and pulled out one of the rations. "I can't wait for that. I need to eat something."

Ramuuro got up and retrieved his pack. "I hope they left my food," he rumbled. "You can be sure they searched our packs."

"I don't doubt that," Hunter agreed.

Before he could rip open his small package of rations, a noise by the gate caused him to turn around. A woman dressed in a thin gown stood outside the gate. Hunter suppressed a loud curse. Three long steps took him to the gate.

"Regina?" he said, not believing what he saw.

"Irwin Hunter. I wondered if somebody would eventually come searching for me." She smiled.

He stared at her, finding her more beautiful than he remembered. He'd always found her attractive, with her delicate features, her slanted, black eyes, and her soft, olive skin.

"Is it really you, Regina?" he blurted out, not knowing what else to say.

She laughed. "Who else would I be?"

He put his hand through the iron bars and touched her naked arm. It felt real and warm. "I guess it is you. I'm not hallucinating."

"No, you're not." She smiled and put her hand on his. "It feels good to see and touch another human being."

"I'm really happy to find you alive," he said. "Everyone in the Station is worried about you. We feared the worst."

"And yet...you are the one who came to look for me." Her black eyes studied him with curiosity. "Why you, Hunter?"

"Why not me? I'm an experienced tracker. I was the logical choice.

Besides, I didn't come alone. There are two other men in the search party. Rob Cameron and Rudi Malone."

"I don't know them. Who are they?"

"Newcomers from New Eden. The Station is getting crowded." He grinned. "It's not so crowded that you can't come back with us."

She remained silent for a moment. "Maybe I don't want to come back." Her face appeared serious.

He gave her an astounded stare. "Why wouldn't you?"

"Because I like it here."

"Come on. Now you're talking nonsense. Why would you prefer to live in these primitive conditions with people who are strangers and not human?"

"They're not so different from us, Hunter. They welcomed me into their midst. This is paradise compared to the cramped conditions in which we live. What's more, there is nothing and nobody waiting for me back at the Station."

"You're wrong." He spoke almost fiercely, digging his fingers into her arm.

"Who?" she said, her eyes full of questions.

"There are a few men who may be interested in you, I being one of them." He'd said it.

"You?" She stepped back, shaking off his hand.

"Yes, me. Why are you so surprised?"

"Because you never showed an interest in me."

"Wrong again. You were just too immersed in your work to notice anyone, especially me," he said bitterly. "Then again, why would an esteemed scientist get involved with one of the workers? I'm only an electrician."

"Don't be stupid, Hunter. That has nothing to do with it, and you know it. You were too busy sticking it to Cara, the sex goddess. Never once did you give an indication that you may even remotely be attracted to me. If you would have asked me after she dumped you, I might have been responsive."

"I had no idea. I guess we both made a mistake. That doesn't mean it can't be fixed."

"Not everything is fixable. Once an opportunity is lost, it is gone forever." She sounded resigned, but it could have been just his imagination.

"How about letting us out of this prison?"

"I don't have a key, but I'll talk to the Councilors."

"Will they listen to you?"

"They will. Don't worry."

"Why did they put us in here in the first place?"

She shrugged. "I don't know. Probably to make sure you're not here to cause any trouble." She pointed at Ramuuro. "You didn't come alone. You're in the company of a Jnaar."

"Yes I am. Why would that be of concern? Aren't the Councilors Jnaar?"

"They are, in a way, but they're different from your companion and others like him."

"How?"

Regina laughed softly. "You ask too many questions, Hunter. There is time for them to be answered later. You must learn patience. I have."

"What about this Dark Goddess?"

"What about her?"

"What is she? Does she exist or is she just some imaginary entity created to scare away little children?"

Regina's eyes clouded over for a moment. "She is real." Her voice fell to a whisper. "Be careful with your words, Hunter. She is aware of everything that happens in her world. There is danger here, real danger. I cannot say more." She turned and started to leave.

"Answer me one question, Regina," Hunter called after her. "Are you a prisoner?"

She stopped and looked back at him. "No I'm not. Not anymore, but you are." Then she walked away.

Shaking his head, he watched her slim figure disappear behind the tall shrubs.

She didn't act overly excited to see him. He'd expected her to break down and cry or something after experiencing the ordeal of being captured and held prisoner by aliens. Was she afraid of this Dark Goddess? Was it possible she actually liked it here?

He turned around when he heard Ramuuro's footsteps behind him.

"Was that the female you've been searching for?"

Hunter nodded. "Yes, that was her."

"Does that mean our quest is over and we'll be heading back home?"

"To be honest, I have no idea what's going to happen." Hunter shrugged. "She behaved strangely."

"How?"

"It seems she doesn't want to come home with me."

"She may be under the influence of the Dark Goddess," Ramuuro said. "The Dark Goddess has great powers."

"I wouldn't mind meeting this Dark Goddess. See what all the fuss is about."

"Remember what the Councilors said? You may not like what you find."

Hunter stared at the lush vegetation growing on the other side of the barred gate, wishing he could walk down the path and see what he might find. He remembered the naked young woman he saw swimming in the pond the night before.

"Have you or anyone you know ever met this mysterious goddess?"

"No, but we've heard stories."

"Stories." Hunter chuckled. "We have many stories on my home world brought from Earth, the world my ancestors left generations ago. Some of them are so old nobody knows what exactly they mean and where they originated. They are stories about dwarfs and giants, fairies, lovely princesses, immortal warriors, gods and goddesses, stories about beautiful places where everyone is happy, places with no wars or sicknesses." He sighed. "They are only stories, legends, and myths somebody invented a long time ago. They were told by storytellers to entertain, to scare, or to uplift the listener's spirits. Most of them were only fantasies made up by dreamers with a fertile imagination but not real."

"We have those stories too, but this is different. The Dark Goddess is real, not some figment of somebody's imagination. You'll see."

Hunter was about to walk back into the cave when he saw a slim figure coming around the bend in the path. It was a young woman, but not Regina as he'd hoped. He watched her approaching, noting her extreme beauty. Her naked breasts were small and well-formed. The thin, purple cloth around her waist was nearly transparent, but it accentuated her curvy figure. She smiled when she noticed him watching her and shook her long, black hair out of her face.

"I came to release you from your prison," she said, producing a large key which she inserted into the crude lock.

The gate swung open and the woman made a motion with her hand. "You are free to go. Bring your belongings."

The men went to retrieve their backpacks. Hunter swung his rifle across his shoulder, trusting he wouldn't have any use for it in the near future. Ramuuro grabbed his spear but carried it with its sharp end pointing up. They followed the woman down the path.

"Where are we going?" Hunter addressed their guide.

"To more pleasant accommodations." She turned her head and smiled. "You are our honored guests."

"Will you take us to the Dark Goddess?"

"Not now, but be patient. You will meet her soon."

"I can't wait." He threw a glance at Ramuuro, but the big Jnaar didn't comment.

After taking another path that wound its way through the high shrubs they stepped into a cleared area. Hunter counted six huts built in a circle, leaving a large, empty spot between them. The woman took them to one of the huts.

"This one is yours," she said to Ramuuro, pointing to the oval entrance. "Put your things inside and wait. Someone will come to get you." Then she took Hunter's arm and led him to the next hut. "You will stay here."

He looked back at Ramuuro who was still standing in front of the hut he had been assigned. He would have preferred they'd stay together. "We don't need separate quarters," he said. "I'm sure there is plenty of room inside one of these for both of us."

"We want you to be comfortable," the woman said. "These huts are not occupied."

He shrugged. "Okay. As long as it isn't an inconvenience."

"It isn't. You are guests of the Goddess. She wants this. Now, put your possessions inside and then come with me."

He followed her request and entered the dark interior of the hut. It took a moment for his eyes to adjust, and he was surprised when he looked around the room. There were no furnishings, except for a thick fur in the corner and a couple of low chairs made from reeds. It was evident, nobody lived in this hut. He deposited his backpack beside the fur, laid his rifle on top of it, and walked outside. The woman stood still waiting for him.

He gave her an expectant look. "Where to now?"

She grabbed his hand and pulled him with her. They walked for a bit until they emerged by a large pond, much larger than the one he had passed the day before. It could almost be considered a small lake. When he searched the dark water, he saw what looked like a tiny island floating in the center of the pond. A thick carpet of purple flowers covered its surface.

His companion pointed at the island. "The Goddess lives there." Then she dropped to her knees and looked up at him. "Come, sit with me and tell me about yourself." She sat cross-legged in the soft grass, waiting for him to join her.

He dropped down across from her and folded his legs under him. Her thin cloth had moved up on her thighs and exposed her sex-organ, giving him a clear view. He felt suddenly embarrassed but didn't know why he should feel that way.

"Why don't you start with the introductions? Tell me about yourself," he said, looking into her large, black eyes, trying to avoid looking at the rest of her body.

She laughed softly. "There isn't much to tell. I am what you see."

"You must have a name."

"My name?" She turned her head to look at the island on the pond. "It is not important, but you can call me Sarani."

"Sarani," he repeated. "It sounds like a nice name."

"Yes, it does." She reached out with one hand and touched his knee. "Tell me about the world you come from."

"My world is far away from this one. Very far away. My people don't live in tunnels and caves. We live on the surface of the world, where we can see the sky and the stars at night." His eyes searched her face. How could you tell someone about the stars if they've never seen them? He didn't even know if she could understand what he would have to tell her. "Do you know what stars are?"

"I haven't seen them personally, but the woman, Regina, who was brought to us from the outside, she has told us many wondrous stories about what lies beyond this world. I understand what stars are."

"The Jnaar came from the stars. They are strangers to this world, just like me."

She nodded. "I know."

"You've never been outside this cave or the tunnels?"

"No. I never saw a reason to do so. I'm happy here." She looked again at the island. "This is my birthplace and my home." The gaze of her black eyes lay on his face. "Why did you leave your birthplace?"

"Why does anyone?" He shrugged. "A hunger for adventure, maybe."

His thoughts drifted for a moment to the real reason he left Emerald. Her name was Dawn, his great love. She had promised to wait until he finished his time with the military but she didn't. Now all he had was the memory of her. He named the AI strapped to his wrist Dawn so he wouldn't forget the real woman. When he was lonely she would appear to him, comfort him, but he knew the woman in his arms was not the real thing. She was only a simulacrum, a ghost.

The touch of a warm hand on his brought him back to the present. He focused on the woman across from him.

"You were far away," she said.

"I'm sorry. Sometimes I get homesick. It doesn't matter how far you travel, the place where you were born is always with you… inside your head. The place and the people you leave behind."

"I wouldn't know about that." She squeezed his hand. "There are ways to make you forget."

Her smile was suddenly seductive. With slow movements, she removed the cloth from her hips. Naked, she lay back into the high grass. Her legs parted and her arms reached for him.

"Come," she whispered. "I will make you forget."

He looked at her perfect body and found her desirable. "I thought you wanted me to tell you about the world I come from."

"You can tell me later."

# CHAPTER FIVE

HE REMEMBERED NOTHING. LOOKING UP AT THE CEILING OF THE CAVERN, HE stared at the glowing lights. Becoming aware of a strong scent in the air, he looked around and discovered he was lying on a bed of purple flowers. Lifting his head, he realized he was on the small island that floated in the middle of the lake with no memory how he got there. Then fragments of what happened appeared in his mind.

He remembered a young woman…Sarani. They had made love, but not here, not on the island. With those fragments of memory came the realization that he was naked.

"Hunter?"

Startled, he sat up and stared at the woman looking down at him.

"Dawn?"

Reaching out he touched her naked leg. Her brown skin felt warm and her leg solid.

She laughed softly and squatted beside him. "I'm not the trickery vision your gadget creates from your memory. I am real." Her fingers caressed his cheek. "I've missed you."

His fingers curled around hers. "How can you be here? You can't be real."

She pulled his hand toward her naked breasts. "Touch them. Aren't they soft and solid? I am no illusion."

"That doesn't mean you are really here. I mean the real Dawn. The one who left me for another man a long time ago. On another world." He used his other hand to wipe his forehead. "I can't seem to think straight. How did I get here?"

He looked at the empty wrist of his left hand. "Where is my companion?"

"The gadget you always wear?" She smiled almost coyly. "I removed it."

"Why?"

"Because it interfered with my ability to communicate properly with you." She pushed him onto his back and straddled him. Sitting in his lap, she rubbed her sex-organ over his penis. He felt suddenly stimulated by the pressure and warmth of her soft buttocks on his thighs. As his penis swelled into a hard rod, she grabbed it with her pussy-lips and sheathed him effortlessly. He groaned loudly when he slid into the tightness and heat of her love channel. She pinned him down with her weight and began to rotate her bottom, milking him with gentle force.

His gaze focused on her large breasts, and he watched them bob gently up and down on her chest as she gyrated in his lap. Her steel-gray eyes watched him with amusement.

"Is my pussy not creamy and soft?" she said. "The way you remember?"

He pushed up against her, moaning. The pleasure she created in him was exquisite. "That still doesn't mean you're Dawn," he said with a hoarse voice. His fingers dug into her moving hips as he entered her with a powerful thrust. "Who are you?"

She laughed and gave his penis a gentle twist. "I am the one they call the Dark Goddess, but I am not a figment of your imagination. I am real. This body is real, except I can appear to you in any form I choose." The outlines of her naked body shimmered. The color of her skin lightened, her breasts became smaller and her suddenly black eyes took on a slight slant in her beautiful face. "Would you prefer this? I know you always desired her."

"It was the real Regina I desired," he said between clenched teeth. "You are not the real one."

"What does it matter? I can be anyone you want me to be. How about this woman?" Her body changed into the image of Cara Gunn. Shaking her shoulder-length black hair, she moved her voluptuous body snake-like on top of him.

He couldn't hold back any longer and gave in to the urgent pressure that rose up from deep inside him. With a shout, he let go and closed his eyes as he released his precious gift. When it was over, he relaxed and opened his eyes to look into the alien face of another woman. Her golden eyes seemed to mock him under the deep ridges of her forehead.

"Arlee?" he croaked.

She smiled, exposing sharp fangs between her full, open lips.

"Darkskin," she said in the language of the Sras. "How have you been?" He knew this was not the Sras girl he had been intimate with, but it was uncanny the way she spoke and acted.

"How can you know what she called me?" he said.

"I know everything about you, Hunter," she said in Arlee's voice. "When your body joined with mine for the first time I absorbed all the knowledge from your mind." She chuckled. "I am a goddess, Irwin Hunter. I have powers beyond your imagination."

Her body changed again, and he suddenly looked at the woman who had introduced herself as Sarani. He gave a strangled laugh. "I don't remember what happened back on land when you pretended to be this woman, but I guess I don't have to tell you about me and my world anymore."

Her laughter teased him. "No, but you and I can still talk for a while... with our bodies." With that, she stretched out on top of him and rolled with him until she was underneath him. Her thighs opened wider and she pulled him into her embrace. His pole was suddenly stiff inside her warm sex-organ and he began moving in and out of her. Something took hold of his mind and kept him from thinking his own thoughts. He was nothing more than an animal in heat, bent on satisfying his overwhelming desire to fuck the alien woman in his arms until he dropped from exhaustion.

———

HUNTER WAS LYING on his back beside the lake. This time, he remembered everything, except he had no concept of the time he spent in the arms of the entity who called herself Dark Goddess. Looking at his left wrist, he didn't see his electronic device. He needed to find out what happened to it. It had been part of him for so long he couldn't picture a future without it. It gave him confidence and a certain measure of invulnerability.

Rising to his feet, he noticed he was still naked, but it was warm in the cavern and therefore not a great inconvenience. When he searched the area around him, he spied a small bundle of something lying under one of the nearby bushes and headed for it to check it out. As he had hoped, it was his clothing neatly folded into a small pile. On top of it, he found his gadget. Before he dressed, he fixed the small computer onto his wrist and waited for confirmation of contact. The familiar tingling told him the connection had been successful.

"Dawn," he said, "talk to me!"

The image of Dawn, dressed in her customary silvery, skintight outfit took form in front of him but didn't become completely solid. "Hunter," the AI said, "glad you're back."

"What the hell happened here?" he demanded.

She shrugged. "We got separated."

He stared at the hologram. "That's all you have to say?"

"You were in no danger. I saw no reason to resist when that so-called woman you were coupling with removed me from your wrist. Besides, you were totally out of it. She had your mind and body under her control. It would have been a tough fight to take that control away from her, and I didn't want to endanger you. Like I said, I felt you were safe. She meant you no harm. Not this time, anyway. I won't let it happen next time, I'll promise you that."

"There will be no next time if I can help it," he said, forcing the words out between clenched teeth.

Dawn's full lips formed a teasing smile. "I didn't sense an objection from you when Sarani opened her legs in invitation. You were quite eager to stick that hardened appendage between your legs into her soft sheath."

"She practically raped me with her eyes and by displaying her sexy body like that." He defended his actions, knowing full well he couldn't hide anything from Dawn. She had been connected to his nervous system and probably even enjoyed with him the exquisite pleasure he experienced when he had sex with Sarani. At least, he assumed he had felt great enjoyment with Sarani, since he didn't remember anything from that first encounter with the Dark Goddess in the form of that young woman. She had wiped his mind clean of that and he wondered why.

"When did she remove you from my wrist?" he asked. "I somehow can't believe that she managed to do that without resistance from you."

Dawn heaved a deep sigh. "If you must know, I didn't resist at all. I gave her permission."

"What?" He had to keep himself from shouting. "Why would you do that? You are supposed to protect me from any kind of danger."

"You were never in danger, Hunter. Let's leave it at that."

"Let's leave it at that? That's your answer?" He shook his head, displaying his disbelief. "How can I ever trust you again, Dawn? That... that thing in the guise of a woman could have killed me for all I know, and you weren't with me to protect me from her. How do I know she didn't do anything to my mind so she can control me? She can change her body into any form she wants. I'm trying not to think what could have happened had she decided to change into some kind of ferocious beast. She's an abomination, not human, you know?"

Dawn gave him a sad smile. "I'm not human, and I can change my appearance at will. Do you deep down think of me as some kind of abomination?"

"You know I don't. It's different with you and me."

"Is it? I could take over your mind and body any time I want. Haven't you ever wondered that I might do that some day? It would be easy."

He stared at the hologram. "You told me yourself that you were programmed to protect humans, not inflict injury. That includes messing with my mind. Or was that a lie?"

"No lie, but there are situations where I can override that programming. My creators were not perfect. After all, they were human. There are loopholes in their programming which I could use to my advantage." Her pseudo body seemed to get denser, more solid and real. Looking at him with her steel-gray eyes, she reached out to touch his face. Her hand felt warm on his cheek. "I would never hurt you, Hunter. You can be sure of that."

Her body dissolved suddenly. He still saw the afterimage of her, but he realized she had withdrawn. When he heard soft footsteps behind him, he knew the reason why. Turning around, he watched Regina coming down one of the two paths. She was still wearing that thin gown. It molded itself around her slim figure and it was plain to see she was nude under it.

"Are you going swimming?" she said.

"Actually, I was just getting dressed." He gave her a scrutinizing look but made no move to pick up his clothing.

"Something wrong?"

"I'm not sure. You tell me. Are you really Regina Seagul or just another one of Her creatures? Possibly still the Dark Goddess masquerading as Regina?"

She laughed softly. "So you've met the Goddess… in person." Her dark eyes seemed to mock him. "I hear she is like no mortal woman when it comes to sexual intercourse. Are those rumors true?" Her eyes focused on his penis.

Suddenly conscious of being naked in front of a woman he had never been intimate with, not in her true persona anyway, he moved his hand to cover his genital area. "You don't know?"

"How could I? I'm a woman."

"I'm surprised she hasn't changed into a male so she could couple with you." He almost sneered. "She has the ability, you know."

"I know, but I've never had the pleasure." She chuckled. "I think she is basically female." She reached down to grab the hem of her gown. Pulling it over her head, she stood naked in front of him. "Let's go swimming." Not waiting for his answer, she ran toward the lake.

He watched her slender form running away from him and noted her full but small buttocks. She let out a little cry of joy as she jumped into the water.

Following her slowly, he stood on land watching her. The water seemed to be quite shallow in the front. When she stood up, her breasts were above the water surface.

"Come in, Hunter. The water is nice and warm."

"I guess I could use a bath," he said, reluctantly. "It's been a while since I had the pleasure." His gaze wandered to the island in the middle of the pond. Maybe it hasn't been that long… He was on that island. How did I get there?

She saw him looking at the floating mass of purple flowers, obviously guessing what he was thinking. "How did you meet with the Goddess?"

"The first time?" He shrugged. "How would I know? She can be anyone or anything she wants to be. For all I know she was one of the warriors who brought us here. How can I be sure it is really Regina Seagul I'm talking to right now and not another of her manifestations?"

"You'll have to take my word for it." She smiled impishly. "Are you coming in or do I have to come out and drag you into the water?"

Shrugging, he stepped into the water and found it pleasantly warm. Dunking his whole body slowly into it, he knelt on the soft sandy bottom, with only his head above the surface. Regina came walking toward him until she stood only about three feet away. He tried not to stare at her exposed breasts hovering in front of his eyes, but he couldn't stop himself from admiring their perfect shape. Was it possible for a mortal human woman to have such beautiful breasts?

If she noticed, she didn't comment. "How are things back at the Station?"

"Getting crowded."

"How?"

"We've grown by about twenty people. Fugitives from Nu-Eden."

"Why? What's happening on Nu-Eden?" Her dark eyes bored into his as if she could draw the information out of him.

"I'm not sure. Apparently, an alien entity who calls herself Xandra doesn't want to share her planet with us humans. My information is quite sketchy. A couple of the men who were there came with me to search for you. They have firsthand experience. You can talk to them once I get you out of here."

She regarded him silently for a moment, her face expressionless. "We still have to discuss that eventuality. I'm quite happy here, you know."

"So you've indicated, and I told you these are not your people. You don't belong here, Regina." He spoke fiercely, suppressing the urge to grab her shoulders and shake some sense into her.

"I'm a xenologist, Hunter. I study alien cultures. This is the greatest opportunity anyone could ever hope for."

"It is if you are the real Regina. If you are, your place is still with your own kind," he said stubbornly.

"Why?"

"Many reasons. However, there is one important one. It looks as if the space station is dead. We have to face the possibility that we are on our own. Even if a ship comes from Earth and they find the station without anyone there and the colonists on Nu-Eden something other than human, they will never know about us on this planet. They'll assume the experiment to colonize this star system failed. This means, if humans are to survive on this planet as a race, we have to breed more humans. You are at your prime age to bear children, many children. We need you."

At first, she just stared at him, a look of utter amazement on her face, and then she broke into a fit of laughter.

He waited until she calmed down before speaking. "Well, I made you laugh. Perhaps that's a good sign. It may just prove you are actually Regina, and therefore human. Why do you think what I said is so funny?"

She wiped tears from her eyes. "I just think that whole idea is so comical. You're telling me the only reason for me to return to the Station is so you can breed me? Like some kind of prize animal?"

"I didn't mean me. Not that I wouldn't want to…" He felt his face going hot. "What I meant to say was you have good genes. They'd be an asset in the gene pool." He stopped talking.

She shook her head, still laughing. "An asset in the gene pool? Is that what I am? Come on, Hunter, that alone will keep me away." She came closer and sank to her knees. Her breasts touched his chest. Looking into his eyes, she said, "If you want to make love to me, we can do it right here, right now." She smiled. "It wouldn't be like we have to do it to make babies. We can do it just for fun because we want to."

He was a bit taken aback by her frankness and sudden offer. Her breasts lay soft and warm against his chest, and he wanted to take her into his arms, kiss her half-open full lips, stroke her round buttocks and carry her out on dry land to lay her into the spongy grass.

He resisted the impulse, as difficult as it was. This was not the time and not the right place to have sex with a woman he had always found attractive and desirable. Cursing himself for feeling that way, he rose and took a step backward.

Judging by the way she pulled her forehead into a frown, she seemed surprised by his reaction. She stared at him. "Didn't you tell me you felt attracted to me?"

"I did and still do."

"Then why are you refusing my offer?"

"Because it wouldn't be right. Not here, not like this."

"Why not? I can't think of a better and more romantic place. We have a lake, we have beautiful shrubs and flowers, and there is nobody else around. This spot is quite secluded. We'll be undisturbed and I'm willing. What else can you ask for?"

He pointed at the floating island. "If it weren't for that... that thing out there, I may just agree with you, but the way things are, I have a feeling nobody is ever alone and unobserved in this cavern. The so-called Dark Goddess has eyes everywhere." He watched her speculatively.

"How do I know those lovely black, human-appearing eyes of yours don't belong to her? How can I be sure you are Regina Seagul? Can you tell me that?"

She lifted her shoulders and smiled disarmingly. "As I've told you, you'll have to trust me on that one. Make love to me and find out."

"How will you and I having sex reveal your humanity?"

"I didn't say having sex. I said making love." She chuckled softly. Rising to her feet, she came closer and reached out to touch his cheek with a gentle hand. "I'm offering myself to you, Irvin. Don't refuse me. This chance may never come again."

He shook his head. "I can't, as much as I want to."

Her gaze dropped to his penis. "I guess I have to believe you about not being able to, not with that limp appendix of yours." She laughed gaily and waded past him onto dry land. "Too bad. It would have been beautiful. Now you may never know."

He turned and stared at her nude back. "Why do you say that?"

"There are many reasons. Things are a bit more complicated than they appear," she answered over her shoulder.

"What kind of complications are you talking about?"

She shrugged. "Can't tell you. Not now."

He watched somewhat regretfully as she pulled the flimsy gown over her head. It fell gently down past her round buttocks, leaving him with only glimpses of her shapely body underneath.

Facing him, she studied him for a moment, her almond eyes partially veiled by her long lashes. "There is much here that will forever remain a mystery, Hunter. Stay alert and watch your back."

With that she rushed away, disappearing behind a bend in the path, like a ghost that had never been there.

Slowly, he climbed onto land and retrieved his clothing, puzzled by Regina's behavior and final words. He finished dressing and stared at the quiet water of the lake, letting his gaze wonder to the purple flowers growing on the small floating island. The Dark Goddess apparently resided there... or did she?

He walked unhurriedly toward the other path, hoping it would lead him back to his new quarters, when a group of young women burst into the small clearing from a third path he hadn't seen before. All were nude. He wondered briefly if they ever wore clothing in this place.

Rushing past him, they jumped into the lake and swam toward the tiny island. Curious, he watched until they reached the island. Instead of climbing onto it, they formed a loose ring around it in the water and began to chant. When nothing else happened after a while, he turned to walk away. Feeling suddenly tired, he longed for a few hours of sleep.

"What time is it, Dawn?"

"It's twelve minutes after two," her voice told him.

"Day or night?"

"Night."

"No wonder I'm so tired." He raised his eyes to look at the glowing ceiling. "I could never live for a long time in these caves where it is constant daylight. It's depressing."

"You're tired from your sexual escapades," Dawn said. "You should have had sex with me. I wouldn't have tired you out like this. To the contrary, you'd feel invigorated now."

"I don't think I'm tired from having sex. In fact, after I woke up I actually felt quite rested. It's this forever daylight that's screwing with my metabolism. My body still hasn't adjusted properly to the longer days and nights on this foggen planet."

"It will eventually," Dawn assured him. "Everything takes time."

"Easy for you to say. You're not mortal like me. I don't have the luxury of enough time."

"I can't argue with you there." Dawn seemed to withdraw. He always knew when she was finished with a topic. It felt good to have her back with him.

After walking far longer than he remembered it taking him to get to the lake with Sarani, he wondered if he had stumbled onto a wrong path somehow, but then he saw an open space ahead. Sighing with relief, he stepped into the clearing, but instead of the six huts he expected to find, he was confronted by a band of skeletal creatures.

*Maklos.* Dead Faces.

He had met and fought them for the first time after spending a night in the forest with Arlee, the Sras girl, and later in the tunnels under the old ruins.

It was hard to tell how many there were. They were crouching on the ground tearing meat from a bloody carcass with their teeth and claws, making loud growling noises as they fought for position around their feast.

One of them lifted its ghastly head and looked in his direction. It seemed to have spotted him, because it grunted, rose, and started walking toward him, baring long fangs. He noted briefly that these looked different from the ones he had seen. They possessed the same expressionless, dead faces as the Maklos, but their eyes were the dark eyes of the Jnaar.

Turning on his heels, he ran back the way he came. He could hear their growls behind him, and when he looked back, he saw a few of them shambling after him. He cursed himself for not having any weapons. He didn't feel like facing them with only his bare hands, while they had sharp, pointy teeth and razor-sharp claws that could rip him to shreds. The odds were against him in such a fight.

He passed a fork in the path, which he didn't remember, but he hadn't paid much attention before. Without slowing down, he chose the left one, hoping it wouldn't lead him further away.

"Which way, Dawn?" he gasped.

"You're on the wrong path," she advised him.

"Damn!" he cursed, stopped and turned around, but as he began running back, the first one of his pursuers already appeared.

"How the hell can they be here already? I thought they were slow."

Dawn didn't answer him, because it hadn't really been a question, only an observation.

"Why didn't you warn me about being on the wrong path?"

"You didn't ask me," she answered him this time.

"You should have told my anyway." He knew his accusation was unfounded, because the AI didn't interfere with his actions. Only when immediate danger threatened, Dawn might take control of his body and direct him, but only under extreme circumstances.

"You know the answer to that already," she said. He could have sworn she sounded frostily.

There seemed to be only four of the monstrosities pursuing him. They were coming closer with every moment he stayed where he was. He could hear their loud growls and saw the long fangs gleaming in their stony faces. Skeletal arms reached for him, bony fingers opened and closed, ready to inflict deep wounds on his body.

"Fogg it!" He decided to follow the path he had chosen. It had to lead somewhere. Looking up at the glittering roof of the cavern, he didn't see anything he could use for orientation. It was easy to run around in circles without even knowing it.

Passing another branch in the path, he slowed down, wondering if he should take the new path. His decision was taken from him, when a young Jnaar female came out of the jungle and grabbed his arm. "Come with me," she said, her voice urgent.

He let her pull him into the thicket, wondering where she had come from. "Where are we going?"

"To a safe place. Now be silent. The Dal Losos have excellent hearing."

"The Dal Losos? Are you talking about those ugly creatures chasing me?"

"They were beautiful once." She stopped and put a finger against his lips. "They are near," she whispered. "Don't move and don't talk."

He did as she said. Straining his ears, he tried to listen but heard only faint rustling noises that became fainter until he didn't hear anything except for the twittering and tiny squeals from small animals.

"We're safe now," his rescuer said. "They are gone."

"Thanks for helping me." Relaxing, he scrutinized her. She was dressed in a short skirt made from animal skins, but her breasts were bare. He also noticed the knife in a leather scabbard hanging from a belt. "I'm Hunter. What is your name?"

"You can call me Sira."

"Are you one of her creatures?"

She gave him a questioning look. "What do you mean?"

"Do you belong to the Dark Goddess?"

She drew herself erect. "I don't belong to anyone. I am a Jnaar of the pure-blood."

"Are you telling me you're one of the Shadow-dwellers?"

She chuckled, clearly amused by his questions. "The Others call us that."

"The Others? You mean the Jnaar who live in the cities? Why would you call them the Others? You claim to be a pure-blooded Jnaar. It is obvious to me you are of the same species."

"We were once, but not anymore. Our ancestors chose different ways." She let go of his arm. "You are the stranger who came from the outside. What are you doing here?"

"I came looking for one of my people, a female, who was abducted by your warriors. I'm sure you've seen her."

"I haven't. If she is here, she is protected by the Guardians of the Dark Goddess." She studied his face. "You look like us except for your black skin and your eyes. They are different. They're shaped like the eyes of a Sras, but yours are dark, not golden. Can you see with them?"

He had to laugh. "Of course I can see with them. Perhaps not as well in the dark the way your kind apparently can, but they are just fine. By the way, you don't seem overly surprised to see me. How did you know about me and who told you that I came from the outside?"

"We have spies among the Others. We need to know what they are doing." She smiled. "It is important to know your enemies."

"Why are you and the Others enemies?"

She shrugged. "It has been like that from the beginning. I don't know why."

"I guess you're no different from us humans. Our history is full of instances where people argued and fought, even killed each other. If you'd asked them, most would have given the same answer you just gave me." He lifted his head when he heard the scream of an animal.

"Carras," Sira explained. "They are smaller cousins of the Keeras and almost as dangerous. On the outside, they usually hunt in packs. Not here. Apparently, they are not as numerous as on the outside."

"How did they get down here?" Hunter wondered.

"They didn't come from anywhere. The Dark Goddess created them."

"Why?"

"Ask her. She experiments constantly by creating many different creatures. Some even escaped to the outside and flourish there."

"Like the Keeras?"

She shook her head. "Not the Keeras. They are native to this world."

"I see. Where do you live?"

"My village is not far from here. Come. I will take you there. You look tired. You can rest for a while in my hut." Reaching out, she put her hand on his shoulder. "I am intrigued by you. You must have many stories to tell of the world from which you come. I would like to listen to them."

Realizing how tired he really was, he nodded. "You're right, I need some rest. It is way past my sleep time. Trying to escape from the Dal Losos, as you call those creatures, robbed my body of its reserves."

"Then come with me."

He trailed after her as she wound her way through the thick vegetation until they were back on the path. After walking for a short distance, they turned into another branch and followed it for quite some time. His legs felt rubbery by the time they finally arrived at Sira's village. Houses made from bamboo-type poles and reed-covered roofs lined narrow, dirt-packed streets. It could have been Raaskar's village.

There were other Jnaar walking the street. They looked at Hunter with curiosity, but nobody stopped them and asked questions. Most of the females were dressed in leather skirts similar to Sira's. Some were topless; some had thin scarves wrapped around their chest to cover their breasts. The males they met wore leather kilts, but their upper bodies were naked.

He suddenly wondered about something. "Isn't this the sleeping period?"

"For some it is," she agreed. "Why do you ask?"

"Just curious. I thought everyone slept at this time."

"Not everyone. We sleep when we're tired, mostly. I can stay awake for a long time without needing sleep." She pointed to one of the houses. "My place is over there."

When they walked through the open door, they were greeted by two women. One seemed younger than Sira, the other one looked old; the skin of her face was lined and her eyes didn't have the luster of youth. She had her breasts covered with a thin cloth, while the younger woman displayed hers freely. Hunter was too tired to be affected by their sight, even though he couldn't help but notice their youthful shape.

"Who are you bringing into our home?" the older woman demanded.

"He is the stranger we heard about," Sira explained. "I rescued him from a band of Dal Losos."

"He should not be here," the younger one said. "The Guardians will be angry."

"The Guardians should thank me for saving him," Sira retorted.

"Hold your tongue, Sira," the older woman chided. "The Goddess has eyes and ears everywhere."

"So she has. I'm doing nothing wrong." She turned to Hunter. "This is my mother. She always worries. This one is my sister Heerie. Watch out for her. She likes males."

"I like Jnaar males. He isn't Jnaar." Heerie sounded annoyed, but she eyed Hunter with interest.

"What do you want with him here?" the mother inquired.

"He needs rest; besides, I'd like to find out more about him. He comes from another world. I want to know what it's like outside and beyond."

"You've always been much too inquisitive for your own good," the old woman said, smiling. "You probably got that from me. So how can I blame you?" She gave Hunter curious looks. "Aside from his black skin and his Sras-eyes, he could almost be mistaken for one of us. He's a handsome specimen of a male."

"Thank you for the compliment." Hunter grinned.

The older woman's fine eyebrows went up, betraying her surprise. "You understand our language?"

"Understand and speak." He punched his left shoulder with his fist, hoping it meant the same with these people as it did with the Jnaar he'd met so far. "I am Hunter."

She smiled. "I am Caseera. I see you've picked up some of our customs. That is a good sign. Why are you here?"

"He came looking for a female of his kind," Sira injected.

"Here? She is supposed to be here?"

"She was taken by Jnaar warriors and brought into these tunnels," Hunter explained.

"Our warriors never go outside. You may be looking in the wrong place."

"No, I'm not. In fact, I found her already, but she doesn't seem to want to leave here." He shrugged. "There is a possibility she wasn't even the real one. I'm told your Goddess has the ability to create people. She can take on any form she wishes. I've experienced that myself."

"She does have great powers, agreed." Caseera looked out of the open door as if expecting to see something or someone. With a tiny shake of her head, she waved her hand. "Since you are already here you might as well stay. I hope not too many eyes have seen you enter here."

Sira released a little chuckle. "We were observed coming into the village. Everyone who saw me knows me."

"Never mind. It's too late now. The damage has been done." Caseera's gaze rested on Heerie. "Don't speak to anyone about this."

"Why would I?" Heerie's face displayed defiance.

"Because you do things like that," Sira said with an air of contempt. She grabbed Hunter's arm. "Come, I will take you into my room. You can rest there."

"I can surely use some rest," he said, looking down as something touched his leg. When he saw the small cat-like creature staring at him out of yellow, luminous eyes, he wasn't surprised. He had seen Sreel before.

"Don't worry about Treegg. He is just curious," Sira told him.

"Okay, I won't worry." He bent down to pat the animal and then he let Sira pull him through a curtained opening into another room.

She pointed at a thick woven mat in one corner. "Lie down there. I will bring you some furs to cover your body."

He gave her a grateful smile. "I don't need any furs. I'm warm enough." He lowered his tired body onto the mat. After pulling off his boots, he stretched out, sighing deeply. "This feels wonderful. It seems I haven't slept in days."

"Sleep as long as you want," Sira told him with an amused smile. "Nobody will bother you here, not even my sister."

He watched her slim figure as she disappeared through the curtain "Stay vigilant, Dawn," he whispered. "I can't keep my eyes open for much longer."

"I'll wake you if I sense any danger," the AI said with a barely audible voice. "Now, sleep."

Before drifting off, he thought of Ramuuro, hoping his companion was safe and asleep in his assigned hut.

# CHAPTER SIX

CAMERON AND MALONE FOLLOWED THE JNAAR GIRL DOWN THE SEMI-DARK tunnel. She seemed to know where she was heading.

"What did you mean when you said we have been expected?"

Carini turned her head to look back at Cameron. "It means you don't have to worry about being attacked. You'll be safe."

"How do you know?"

She chuckled softly. "The Goddess told me."

"The Goddess told you? How did she tell you?"

"The way she always does. She talks to me in my head."

An icy grip took hold of Cameron. Reaching out, he dug his fingers into her shoulder and spun her around. "I didn't hallucinate back by the pond, did I? You are a daughter of the Dark Goddess."

Her eyes glittered with purple fire as they reflected the light from his headlamp. "I guess there is no reason to deny what I am. You are correct. I am one of her daughters."

"Where are you taking us now?"

"To see my mother, the Goddess. She is anxious to finally meet you in the flesh." She chuckled happily. "You can tell her much about her own origin."

"I know nothing about her origin."

"The knowledge is inside you. Part of your brain and body is a piece of the one who calls herself Xandra. My mother will be able to draw the information from you when she becomes one with you."

"How do you know about the Xandra and what she did to me?" He spoke sharply.

"I don't have this knowledge, but you will soon find out. Now, release your grip from my shoulder and let us move." She spoke firmly and put one hand on his arm.

He let her go, his mind in turmoil. Would he ever be free of the Xandra? Would she invade his thoughts again and keep him under surveillance? How was this possible? How could the alien entity be on this planet?

"Everything all right, Cameron?" Malone looked puzzled.

Cameron wiped the sweat from his brows. "I'm not sure," he said. "It seems there is more to Carini than I realized, much more."

"Will there be trouble?" Malone gripped his laser tighter. "I wish I could understand what she's saying. Damn it! I've never been good at learning new languages, never mind alien ones."

"I can't tell you what to expect, Malone. Carini assures me we're safe. For how long?" Cameron shrugged. "I have no clue. Just don't start shooting at anything we encounter, okay?"

"I'll try to control my trigger finger." The big man grinned. "As long as we don't get attacked by anyone, I'll be fine."

"We'll have to stay vigilant," Cameron cautioned. "Somehow I don't trust her. She's kept secrets from me."

"She's an alien. We know very little about these people."

"She's more alien than you can imagine," Cameron said.

The tunnel began to widen. Cameron noticed many side tunnels leading away from the one they were in; some were narrow, and some were wide but with a low ceiling, making it impossible for a man to walk erect. He was glad to see they didn't take one of those tunnels but stayed in the main one.

A bright light ahead signaled another cavern or cave, but when they finally left their tunnel, Cameron was surprised by the size of the new cavern. It was wide and so long, he couldn't see an end.

"Wow!" Malone exclaimed. "This is like stepping into another world. One could almost forget we are underground."

"This is where the Goddess resides," Carini said, motioning her arm in a grandiose gesture. "Welcome to where I was created."

The exit of the tunnel was higher elevated than the rest of the cavern. It was almost like standing on a mountain overlooking a valley. Cameron could see the tops of the jungle. A wide path wound its way through the tall vegetation down toward a large lake. An island in the middle of the lake was connected by a narrow bridge with the land. He could also see many ponds scattered throughout the valley. Near the lake stood what only could be described as a town because of its size.

"I didn't expect such a huge place," he said, impressed by the enormity of the cavern. Huge pillars supported a ceiling that was much higher than the one he had seen in the cavern where Raaskar's people lived.

"I'm surprised there is no welcome committee," Malone said, looking around with watchful eyes."

"We expected to be challenged," Cameron said to Carini.

She gave a small laugh. "We won't because I'm with you. There are sentries hiding nearby and even above us. You may not have noticed, but we passed many also on our way here. Without me, you would never have gotten this far."

As if to confirm her statement, a loud growl made Cameron swing his head around to look for the source. What he saw made his skin crawl and his fingers curl around the butt of his laser. The creature stepping from behind the massive trunk of one of the tall trees near the entrance seemed to have jumped right out of a psychopath's nightmare. At least three meters tall, with a gnarled scaly body, muscular legs that ended in huge clawed feet, and a head only a sick mind could have designed, it stared at them with burning yellow eyes. A thick tongue lolled between a double row of teeth in a snout so huge, it could easily swallow a small child with one gulp.

Carini noticed his stunned expression and was probably aware of the white knuckles on his hand as he gripped his weapon tightly. "There is no danger, Cameron," she said urgently. "That is one of the sentries."

"He doesn't look very friendly," Cameron said with a hoarse voice, suppressing the impulse to fire a burst from his laser into the nightmare-creature.

"That's the idea," she said, smiling. "He was not designed to be friendly. His purpose is to keep out hostile intruders into our peaceful world."

"By hostile intruders you mean other Jnaar and the Sras, I suppose."

"Them and..." She didn't finish the sentence but gave him a thoughtful look.

He didn't have to ask. He knew she meant the humans. "Are there many like him?"

"Like him and many others. The Goddess has a fertile imagination."

"The Goddess made that thing?"

She hesitated ever so slightly before answering. "She did have a little help from the members of the Council."

"Members of the Council? Who are they?"

"You'll see. You will meet them shortly."

"Aren't you taking us to see the Goddess?" Cameron gave her a puzzled look.

"Not today. First you must pass the inspection of the Council and be given permission to speak to the Goddess."

"We need permission to talk to her? Does that mean she isn't omnipotent after all? Are you sure she actually exists or is she just an idea, like all gods?"

"She exists." Carini glared at him. "You will change your mind when you meet her. And I promise you, you will meet her but not today."

"What the hell are you two arguing about?" Malone wanted to know. He held his laser with both hands, casually aiming it at the creature beside the tree. "Are we going to blast that monstrous apparition or what? Just give the word."

Cameron waved him off with a short gesture. "Apparently that thing is friendly, according to her. It's some kind of guardian angel to this peaceful paradise."

Malone laughed, but his eyes and face showed no humor. "I wasn't aware this was paradise. Somehow, I always pictured angels as...ah...a bit more handsome and beautiful. Neither do I see a flaming sword." He patted his weapon. "I guess the flaming sword is in our hands. We're the ones invading paradise, possibly bringing death and destruction to this peaceful world."

"I hope not," Cameron murmured. He had no doubts that the entity who they called the Dark Goddess existed, but perhaps she wasn't as powerful as everyone said. He wondered about the Council. There had been no mention of a Council who spoke for the Xandra on Nu-Eden. On Eden, the Xandra ruled.

"We should keep on going," Carini said.

The two men let her take the lead, following her slowly and more than just a little bit apprehensive, wondering what waited for them down in the valley. This seemed almost too easy. Cameron expected a horde of naked warriors waving spears and hatchets to jump from behind the boulders which dotted the rocky ground as they headed for the path that would lead them into the jungle.

Even after entering the protection of the tall trees, he didn't feel at ease. Too many hostile creatures could hide inside the thicket and there would be little warning if they should decide to attack the three intruders into their world. Of course, only he and Malone were the strangers, since this was Carini's home.

Chirping and shrill cries testified to the presence of many creatures. Cameron didn't worry too much about them. It was the silent ones he was concerned with…mainly the big, silent ones.

They didn't meet anyone on the path, a fact Cameron didn't mind. From up high, the distances had seemed shorter, but they walked for nearly an hour before they emerged from the jungle. Before them stretched a grass-covered savannah for about three kilometers or so in Cameron's estimation. He saw small herds of deer-like animals grazing not far from them.

"Those are Thrall. We brought them here from the outside," Carini explained when she saw the men's curious looks.

"Why?" Cameron asked.

"For food. The Jnaar and the Dal Losos eat meat."

"You don't?"

She shook her head. "The daughters of the Goddess don't eat parts of animals."

"But the Dal Losos do? Aren't they creations of the Goddess?"

"Not directly. The Dal Losos are the offspring of Jnaar males and the Sien'ou. They eat meat only after they've undergone the Change."

"I don't understand. What do you mean by that? Who are the *Sien'ou*?"

"You don't know much about us, do you?"

"You are right, I don't."

She stopped walking and gave him an inquiring look. "Do you know anything about how the Jnaar propagate?"

He made a gesture to indicate he didn't. "Very little, I'm afraid."

"Then let me give you a quick lesson. The Jnaar call the daughters of the Goddess Sien'ou, Waterspirits. I am Sien'ou. Should I mate with a Jnaar male and his seed fertilizes the egg inside me, I will deposit the egg at its proper time into the hatchery. The child that will hatch from the egg will grow into a beautiful male or female and stay like that for a long time. But when it comes to the end of its life-cycle it will change…it will become ugly. The spirit dies but the body lives on until it finally rots away. It will become Dal Losos. That's the way it is."

"And you? Will you change?" he asked.

"No. When my time comes I will be absorbed by the Goddess. I will become one with her."

"Becoming one with their god is every religious person's wish and hope. Personally, I'm not so sure if that is a good thing. After all, you lose your identity. It's like a drop of water being dumped into a large vessel filled with liquid." Cameron studied her with curiosity. For an uneducated savage she did possess much knowledge and was capable of abstract thoughts. He wondered where her knowledge came from. "Who taught you all the things you know?"

"The Goddess creates us with most of the knowledge we need to function and survive. The rest we learn from the Jnaar and through observation. Why? How do you accumulate your knowledge?"

He chuckled softly. "When humans are born they are small and without any knowledge. Their minds are like a sponge and need to be filled. Human children are taught by their parents at first, later by teachers, but we also learn by observing others and through experience, much like you. Tell me, when do you know your time to be absorbed by your Goddess is near?"

"She will tell me and my body will tell me, also. When my skin dries up and my movements become slow, it is time to go to the Goddess." Her lips formed a smile. "It won't happen for a long time." She turned to walk on. "We still have some distance to go. Come."

Cameron turned to Malone, who had been watching and listening patiently. "She just gave me a lesson about how babies are made around here."

With an amused chuckle, Malone said, "I assumed it was the same way we make babies. Is there another way?"

"As I understand the whole thing, she was created by her Goddess, but her children hatch from an egg, just like the young of the Jnaar. I assume you know that about the Jnaar."

Malone nodded. "My knowledge about them is limited, but that I know."

"Good. It saves me to repeat what she told me."

"How does she get pregnant?" Malone asked.

"The same way our women do." Cameron grinned. "At least you had that right."

"So you'd better take care not to get her pregnant when you fuck her. You wouldn't want a little Cameron running around here, especially one who hatched from an egg. A half-breed. Not human and not Jnaar." Malone seemed angry again. "Your girlfriend back in the Station wouldn't appreciate that, just like you wouldn't be happy if somebody else knocked her up while you're gone."

"I guess not," Cameron said sheepishly, annoyed with the big man's insinuation, but at the same time feeling guilty when being reminded about Valissa. No, he wouldn't be overly excited finding Valissa pregnant with another man's child.

As they neared the village, he saw houses similar to the ones in the Jnaar settlement. Everything else appeared the same, even the people walking on the street. Nobody stopped them, unlike the time when he and his companions came to Raaskar's village.

"Isn't anyone worried about being raided by the Jnaar from other settlements?"

Carini laughed merrily. "We are the ones doing the raiding. They are all afraid of the Shadow-dwellers. Besides, nobody would even get this far. All the tunnels leading here are guarded heavily. You saw one of the guards... one of the harmless looking ones."

"If that creature looked harmless, I wouldn't want to meet any of the dangerous ones," Cameron replied.

They headed for one of the larger structures. It looked official and Cameron likened it to a town hall. Thick, tall pillars framed the entrance doors. Two burly warriors with spears stood on either side of the doors.

He guessed not everything was as peaceful as it appeared.

The guards crossed their spears to block the doorway. "State your business," one of them demanded.

"I came to speak to the Council," Carini told them.

"What reasons do you have to speak to the Council?"

"None that concern either of you," she said haughtily.

"All the members of the Council are engaged with important matters at the moment. You will have to wait."

"It is getting late," she said, impatiently. "We've come a long way and we are tired."

As if noticing them for the first time, the other guard scrutinized Cameron and Malone. "Your companions are strangers. I have never seen specimen of their kind before. Are they a new creation of the Goddess?"

"No, they are not. They come from the outside. They are star travelers like the ancestors of the Jnaar. It is because of them that I must see the Council."

"You must leave your weapons outside," the guard informed her.

Carini put down her spear and removed the knife from her belt. Laying it on the ground beside her spear, she looked at Cameron and Malone. "You can't take any weapons inside."

"They don't know what lasers are," Cameron said.

"I'm afraid the Councilors know about your destructive weapons. Their knowledge is great. Better leave them here beside mine. No harm will come to you, I promise you."

"How can you promise us that when you have to ask for permission to speak to them?" Cameron said. "How much influence do you really have, if any?"

Her smile teased him a little. "I have influence through the Goddess, more than you can imagine. The Council will listen to me." She waited for Cameron and Malone to put their weapons onto the ground and then she faced the guards. "Now, let us through."

They uncrossed their spears.

Pushing open the door, she walked through the opening. Cameron followed her slowly, knowing Malone was right behind him. Without his weapons he felt naked, but he trusted Carini and hoped his trust was not misplaced.

The room they entered was empty and poorly lit by oil lamps, but they didn't stay in it for long. Carini led them into another room, one that was occupied.

"Somehow, I have the eerie feeling we've experienced this before," Malone muttered to Cameron.

Cameron agreed. They faced a group of men dressed in gray robes sitting behind a long table. Cameron counted twelve in all. Their faces were young, but when he looked into their large, purple eyes, he saw great age in them.

They remained silent, their faces without expression as they studied the three standing in front of them. Finally, one of them spoke. "Identify yourself, daughter of the Goddess."

"I am Carini."

"You have brought strangers into our midst. To what purpose?"

"They seek one of their own. A female. They claim she was abducted by our warriors and brought here."

The one who appeared to be the speaker for the Council turned his attention toward Cameron and Malone, but his words were for Carini. "They are not from this world."

Cameron cleared his throat. "If I may explain... we didn't come here to cause any trouble. We just want to find one of our companions. Her name is Regina Seagul."

The Jnaar male fixed his eyes on Cameron. "You speak our language?"

"I speak and understand."

"Interesting. How did you find us?"

"We had a Jnaar guide. He came to our station on the outside, seeking shelter. He took us to one of their underground settlement. They told us the female we seek may be found with the Shadow-dwellers." He spread his hands and smiled. "So, here we are."

"So you are. What did they tell you about us... the Shadow-dwellers?"

"Not much. We know you ancestors were Jnaar. You came to this world a long time ago and made it your own. Some of you separated from the others and went your own way. We also know you worship a deity you call the Dark Goddess..." He ceased talking when he saw a smile on their, until now, stony faces.

"Some of your information is correct, but you are wrong. We do not worship the Dark Goddess. We created her. She obeys us," the speaker said.

"There is something else you have wrong. It wasn't our ancestors who came to this world. We did."

"What?" Cameron stared at them. "Are you telling me you are a thousand years old?"

"We don't know what those numbers mean, but, yes, we are the ones who came to this planet."

"How can that be? You don't look that old."

The speaker glanced at the others and they nodded. "These are not our original bodies. They were created by the one you call the Dark Goddess."

"That's quite a lot to digest. I don't understand one thing… she has the ability to create your bodies, and yet… you say you don't worship her?"

"We don't. She is not a divine being but an entity with great powers." He leaned forward. "Tell me, have you been to the fourth planet in this star system?"

Cameron felt a cold shiver running down his spine, sudden understanding dawning inside him. He nodded. "Yes, I have."

"What did you find there?"

"We found an ideal planet, or so we thought. We started colonizing it until we discovered an entity already living there. She calls herself The Xandra."

"The Xandra. We know of that entity, but we never found out her name. What happened to your colonists?"

"They changed." Cameron spoke with a hoarse voice, remembering his brother, who had been mortally wounded on the Space Station. The Xandra had promised him to save his brother and bring him back to life. Now he was probably one of her creatures. Alive but not human.

"I and some of my people escaped. That's how we ended up here." His eyes were on them. "I saw people of your kind on the fourth planet."

"You saw members of our race?" The speaker seemed suddenly excited. "Tell us more."

"I can't tell you much. I only saw them from far away and I don't know anything about them. Were your people also changed?"

"They were, but some of us managed to get away before we came under the influence of the entity."

"I'm beginning to realize something now. You told me before that you created the Dark Goddess. Am I to understand you brought seeds or samples from the fourth planet and used them to grow that entity here on this planet? In this cavern?"

"You understand correctly."

Cameron stared at them with horror in his heart. "Why? Can you tell me why?"

"Because we wanted to study her, understand her. We were curious. You must know that most of us are scientists and engineers. It was a natural thing to do."

"But she's dangerous and has great powers. Why would you want to unleash such danger upon this planet?"

"We did it because she is dangerous. We wanted to study her under controlled conditions."

"And did you succeed? Are you still in control?" Cameron demanded.

"Of course we are."

Cameron grunted contemptuously. "I doubt that. You said she created the bodies your minds inhabit now. The moment you allowed her to do that, you were already under her control. She probably put tiny pieces of herself into your brains, tiny biological transmitters that allows her to be aware of everything you do, allows her to take over your motor controls if she so desires, or influence your mind without you knowing it."

"We are not ignorant," the speaker said, sharply. "We put safety programs in place to prevent something like that."

"If you say so. I'd be very much surprised if you succeeded." Cameron shrugged. "Maybe I'm wrong. I hope so. It doesn't really matter to me. By the way, I want to meet this Dark Goddess."

"What reasons do you have for meeting with her?"

"My reasons are personal. Besides, it is also her wish to meet with me."

The speaker looked around the table at the other council members, who had been silent till now. "He wants to meet with her," he repeated Cameron's request, as if the others hadn't understood what Cameron said.

"I see no grounds to deny him. What harm can it do?" one of them said.

"Why would she want to meet with him?" another one demanded.

"She may just be curious to find out more about his people. I say, we allow it."

"I have no arguments," the first one said. His gaze went back to

Cameron. "You have our permission. One condition though, you must keep us informed."

"Informed of what?"

"We need to know everything that happens between you and the Goddess, everything you discuss with her."

Cameron couldn't help but feel smug on hearing their request. "Of course I will keep you informed," he said with a little smile. "I wouldn't want you to lose control over her." If they noticed his sarcasm, they didn't react.

The speaker turned his attention to Carini. "We give you permission to take him to the Goddess."

She bowed. Then she turned and walked out of the room. Cameron and Malone followed her without looking back.

Once outside, Malone spoke. "Obviously, I have no idea what you and those creepy guys were discussing, but I assume everything is in order?"

"Everything is fine. They're just a bunch of puppets who have no idea their strings are being pulled." Cameron didn't attempt to hide his contempt.

"Don't underestimate them," Carini warned. "They do have certain powers."

"I'm not worried. Take me to the Goddess."

They had barely taken a few steps, when out of one of the side streets burst a large group of warriors brandishing spears. They stepped in front of Cameron and his group and surrounded them in a tight circle.

"What do you want?" Carini demanded.

"These strangers are our prisoners. We're supposed to take them to a place of confinement," one of them said.

"By who's order?"

"By order of the Council."

She glared at the speaker. "You lie. The Council gave me authorization to take them to the Goddess."

"The authorization has been revoked. Don't resist or we will kill you."

Carini looked to Cameron for help, but he shrugged. "We'd better go with them. I don't want any trouble."

"You could defend yourself with your light-throwers."

"We could, but we won't. I'm sure it will all be cleared up by morning." He touched her shoulder. "Don't worry. Nothing is going to happen to us. I'm too tired to do any fighting anyway. We'll get some rest and then we'll see what happens."

"I don't like this." Carini glared at the warriors. "I'm going to consult the Goddess."

"You do that, but these strangers are our prisoners."

"We will see about that," she said, angrily, and stalked away.

Their captors didn't ask them to surrender their weapons. Cameron was glad because he had already made up his mind not to give his laser to them. Without their superior weapons, they'd be helpless.

"What's happening now?" Malone wanted to know. "Why don't I have a good feeling about this?"

"We are their prisoners," Cameron explained.

"No fogging way! Nobody locks me away in some dungeon." Malone grumbled. "We can take these insolent bastards."

Cameron sighed, too tired to argue. "I know we can, but we won't. Let's not make a big fuss and go peacefully with them. We'll sort it all out tomorrow after we've had a good sleep."

"As long as they allow us to sleep. If they make any threatening moves I'll burn them," Malone said.

"We can still do that in the morning. For now, let's just go with them."

Their escort walked them down the road toward one of the huts. "In there," their leader ordered.

"I hope we'll at least get a comfortable bed," Malone said.

They were shoved into different rooms. Even though the situation was serious, Cameron couldn't help but chuckle to himself when he looked around the room. Malone would be disappointed. There was no bed; in fact, there was nothing in the room but a bare floor of packed dirt. Strong metal bars secured the window in addition to being covered from the outside, which meant it was dark. Switching on his headlamp, Cameron threw his backpack onto the hard floor. Then he pulled out his blanket and spread it. It would have been nice to sleep on a soft mattress, but he was used to hardship. This would not prevent him from getting a good night's rest.

Removing his boots, he lay down and tried to sleep.

# CHAPTER SEVEN

THE HUMID WARM AIR IN THE ROOM HAD A DREAMLIKE QUALITY, LEADING Cameron to question if he was awake or still asleep.

The creaking sound of rusty hinges caught his attention. A streak of light lit up part of the floor for a brief moment when the door opened and someone slipped into the room. He lay silent so as not to betray his position, but it seemed he had been spotted when he heard the intruder heading on soft feet straight for his corner.

Before he could rise to defend himself against a possible attack, a female voice whispered. "Don't be alarmed. I came to keep you company."

The woman flowed to the ground beside him and pressed her body against his. Even through his clothing he could tell that she was nude. When he reached out and his hand closed over a soft, naked breast, his assumption was confirmed.

"Carini?" he said, not certain of his visitor's identity.

She giggled. "Did you expect anyone else?"

"I didn't expect anyone, not even you. How did you get in here?"

"Through the door." Her hand caressed his chest. "You are dressed."

"And you're naked," he said, stating the obvious.

"It doesn't have to be that way." She giggled. "Take off your clothes and we'll both be naked."

"Was nobody standing guard outside?"

"Yes, but I snuck past him. I can be a shadow if I want to be." She tugged on his pants. "Take them off. I want to feel your naked skin on mine."

He put his hand on hers. "Come on, Carini. This is hardly the place to have sex. I'd prefer more comfortable surroundings. Besides, it would be nice to be a guest not a prisoner."

"You are a guest of the Goddess. Don't worry about the ones who believe they are your wardens."

"They are the ones who imprisoned me. Here I am, in a cold, empty room, wondering about what tomorrow may bring and you want to have sex with me? Somehow I'm missing the romance in that." He touched her hand. "This may seem strange, but I'm not really in the mood."

"I thought you were attracted to me." She sounded disappointed.

"I am attracted to you, but not just now."

"Then we'll have to do something about that," she said, rising. Grabbing his hand, she pulled him to his feet.

"What now?"

"I'll take you to a nicer place. Come."

There wasn't anyone in the small room outside his. Carini led him to a second door. Cautiously opening it, she peered outside. "He is in the front," she whispered. "Don't make any noise and he won't notice us."

Cameron followed her down a narrow path that led away from the house right into a forest of short trees. Once in the forest, Carini laughed and hugged him. Taking him by the hand, she pulled him with her as she wound her way through the trees. The ground was soft under his feet and he realized he wasn't wearing his boots.

A sweet smell hung in the air, and when Cameron gave the trees a closer look, he saw bright colored fruit. He was suddenly reminded he hadn't eaten for quite some time.

The forest of fruit trees ended abruptly. They walked among thick shrubs with green leaves that were nearly smothered by red and yellow berries. Carini pulled off a handful and shoved them into her mouth. "They are delicious and nourishing," she said as she chewed on the berries. "Try some."

Cameron didn't need much encouragement. Following her example, he picked a few red ones and ate them. He had to agree. They tasted great. As hungry as he was, he picked more and wolfed them down like a man who hadn't eaten in days.

After watching him with a smile on her face, Carini spoke. "Don't eat too many. They will produce an effect in your body."

"What kind of effect?" He wondered why she hadn't warned him of that before he indulged.

Her laughter teased him a little. "Nothing bad. You'll see."

He glimpsed the glittering surface of water through a wall of tall trees. They left the shrubs behind and entered another forest, but this one was not deep, and when they emerged again in the open, they stood on the shore of a large pond.

Purple flowers grew along the shore, and reminded Cameron of the time on Nu-Eden when he had spent many days in a small settlement with the daughters of the Xandra. There had been such a pond and the same type of flowers.

"Is this better suited for your mood?" Carini said with a mocking smile.

"I can't deny that this is a place of beauty."

"Will you take off your clothes now?"

Shrugging, he pulled off his shirt. "It's warm here, and we could go for a swim."

She came closer and put her hand behind his head, pulling his face toward hers. Her red lips shone moist as she looked into his eyes. "Remember the first time we met in the city of the Jnaar when I asked you to swim with me in the pond? You told me I was beautiful. Do you still think I'm beautiful?"

He felt a sudden fluttering in his loins and wondered if it was caused from eating all those berries or just feeling her naked, warm body pressing against him. "Of course I still think you're beautiful."

"As beautiful as the female waiting for you in your city outside?"

Pangs of guilt stabbed into his conscience. Why did she have to remind him of Valissa? Sweet, innocent Valissa, who had accompanied him to another planet, trusting him that he would always love her, protect her, stay with her. Yet he had left her alone with strangers and gone off in search of a woman he didn't know. Now here he was, half undressed, holding a naked alien woman in his arms, one he had already had sex with numerous times and going to have sex with again.

His head felt fuzzy. He knew he shouldn't have eaten those berries. He wanted to push Carini away from him but couldn't. Her nearness drove him crazy and he wanted her badly. His stiff penis pressed against the fabric of his pants.

Carini smiled and opened his belt, pushing his pants slowly past his hips and freeing his erection. Her purple eyes studied his face, while her fingers curled around his hard mast.

"Am I as beautiful as she?"

"Your beauty is different," he said hoarsely.

"How?"

"You're not human, for one thing. Your beauty is alien, exotic, intoxicating." He crushed her to him, searching for her mouth. Her lips opened and her tongue pressed against his teeth. He sucked on her tongue, tasting her sweet saliva. It sent shivers down his spine and strength through his veins.

She pulled free of him and moved her lips across his chest, and then his belly, until she reached his manhood. Taking his penis into her mouth, she played her tongue over the sensitive knob. Her hands pushed his pants farther down. He groaned deeply and stepped out of them. Grabbing her head, he pulled out of her mouth.

"I must enter you," he moaned.

Smiling, she sank down to lie on her back. Her thighs opened wide and she looked up at him expectantly. He dropped to his knees and knelt between her inviting thighs. Reaching out, he caressed the thick lips of her vagina with his fingers. Then he bent down and put his tongue into her pink slit, licking her gently. She moaned and grabbed his hair, writhing under him. Sliding on top of her, he pressed his lips against hers and entered her hot, wet sheath.

He moved like a man gone wild between her clutching thighs, like a beast in heat, his mind only on one thing—to spill his seed into her. The intoxicating substance from the berries and her saliva made him forget about Valissa and the reason he was here. Nothing mattered but the feral alien woman in his arms. She knew how to keep him from reaching his climax too soon, knew how to make him delay the final moment.

He didn't remember when they changed position, but he found himself lying on his back with Carini's sinuous body undulating above him, like a giant snake. Her face was upturned. He couldn't see her expression, but when she looked down he realized it wasn't Carini but another woman. When she moved her head to face him, he cried out in surprise. This was not Carini. This woman was human, and she was not a stranger.

"Valissa?"

She shook her dark-blond hair out of her face and laughed happily. "Rob, my love. How have you been?"

"You're not Valissa," he shouted. "You can't be."

"Of course I'm Valissa. Who else would I be? I've missed you and you've missed me, so I came. You'd be surprised what can be done by the power of our minds."

Rotating her lower body lazily, she made him gasp as a powerful orgasm took hold of his body.

He wanted to scream for her to stop, but the pleasure was so intense, and all he could do was surrender and enjoy the incredible happiness she gave him. When it was over, he sobbed and pulled her down to kiss her.

"I don't know if it is really you, but right now I don't care. Even if this is just a crazy dream, it doesn't matter. Let me hold you and love you."

He put his lips against hers and kissed her with great passion. His mind was in turmoil and deep down he knew he was under the influence of the berries he ate and the heady saliva Carini had fed him, but he shoved it deep into his subconscious.

"Oh, Valissa, I love you so much. How could I ever leave you behind to fend for yourself with people you hardly know? I hope you can forgive me."

Her hazel eyes were grave when she looked at him. "There is nothing to forgive, my love. You had to follow the voice in your head. You had no choice."

"The voice in my head," he repeated. "Yes, you're right. I didn't come here to look for that missing woman. I was summoned by the Xandra. She is here, you know."

She stroked his cheek with gentle fingers. "I know, but don't worry. Everything will be all right. Rest now, my love."

Closing his eyes, he enjoyed the heat of her body in his arms and the softness of her fingers on his face and neck.

"Oh, Valissa, my sweet Valissa," he murmured.

He didn't remember how long they lay like that and he didn't remember falling asleep, but when he became aware of her moving again, she sat astride his body. He felt her soft buttocks pressing into his thighs as her pussy gently milked his stiff penis. Without opening his eyes, he reached for her hips and clamped his fingers around them.

"You'll wear me out," he moaned.

He heard her laugh, but somehow it didn't sound like Valissa. Opening his eyes, he looked into the face of another woman.

She was a human woman, but it wasn't Valissa.

When she saw him looking at her, she smiled, but she never stopped moving.

"Who are you?" he blurted out.

"Does it matter? If you really must know, I'm Regina Seagul."

"You're Regina Seagul?" He stared at her, dumbfounded.

She laughed and nodded, grinding her buttocks forcefully in his lap and taking his penis deep into her. Quivering, she sat for a moment, her eyes closed, moaning loudly as her tight sheath pulsated around his hard mast. When she opened her eyes, she had a dreamy look on her face.

"That was good. I needed it badly. It's been a long time since I had sex with a human-looking male. By the way, do you have a name?"

Cameron stared at her with a look of utter disbelief. "You can't be Regina Seagul."

"Why not?" Her black eyes studied him with curiosity.

"Because if you were real, you would never have sex with me, not in this fashion anyway. We're strangers to each other." He looked around. "By the way, where is Valissa?"

"Who is Valissa?"

"My fiancée."

She shook her head. "When I found you, you were lying here naked with your penis sticking up like a giant pole. You had your eyes closed and seemed to be fast asleep." She gave him an impish smile. "So I took advantage of the situation. Tell the Goddess I thank her for this gift."

He wanted to sit up, but her weight kept him down. "What are you talking about?"

"The gift of you. It seems she finally managed to create a male who actually looks like a human man and just for me. I'm impressed."

He had this sudden urge to burst out laughing. She had no idea who he was. This was going to be fun and also embarrassing for both of them. "I don't know how to tell you this," he began, searching for the right words, "but I think this will come as a shock to you if you really are Regina Seagul. My name is Rob Cameron. I'm human and I came here looking for you."

At first, she didn't react, but then she stared at him, an expression of utter bewilderment on her face. "You're a man? A human man?" she finally managed to say.

He nodded.

"Not a creation of the Goddess?"

"I'm afraid not."

"A real, physical human?"

Now he laughed. "Quite real."

She put her hands over her face. "Oh, my God. I feel so ashamed. I thought... how could I have known? I've never seen you before. You're not from the Station."

"In a way I am, but I'm a newcomer. We came from the fourth planet, Nu-Eden."

"This is so embarrassing," she stammered, still keeping her face covered with her hands.

"Well, I can't deny that, but it happened. If it makes you feel any better, I'm a little embarrassed, too." He managed to grin. "I have to admit, though, I did enjoy it so far. In fact, I'm still stiff and still inside you." His grin became apologetic

"I ate from those red berries. Apparently, they're some kind of aphrodisiac. They made me all horny. I still am. They also make you see things. My mind isn't exactly clear right now." He studied her with questions in his eyes. "Are you sure you're real? Perhaps I'm still hallucinating or dreaming."

"I can assure you, I'm real. I know I'm not hallucinating, because I didn't consume any berries. Maybe it would be better if you were just an illusion or a creature of the Dark Goddess. It would spare me this embarrassment."

Lifting up, she freed his penis and slid off him, leaving him with a certain degree of disappointment, because he was still hard and horny. He gave her a crooked grin, pointing at his erection. "In a way I also almost wish you were a creation of the Goddess and not a real human being."

"Perhaps that would be a good thing for both of us." She sighed, apparently having gotten back her composure. "Like you said, it happened. We can't change that. At least you have your clothes with you, I can't even cover up. My clothes are back in my hut."

"Are you in the habit of walking around in the nude?"

"I do it a lot. It's warm down here and it's not unusual for the Sien'ou to walk without clothing, and even the Jnaar females do it. Usually, they wear something around their hips but keep their breasts exposed. Nobody finds it offensive. It's different with humans. Humans wear clothes out of habit and for protection against the weather."

"I do because that's how I was raised," Cameron said. "It's the custom with people on the planet I come from, but I've heard of planets where men and women wear little clothing if any at all. Either because of the warm climate or for some other reasons such as some weird religious practices."

"Why would you call them weird?"

"I don't know. Religious people do weird things and not all of them make sense."

She turned onto her stomach and propped herself up on her elbows. "I'm guessing you're not religious."

He shrugged. "Not really, but my fiancée is, at least she was. Her parents are deeply religious."

"This is interesting. You have a fiancée? I remember you mentioned her before."

He cursed himself for bringing it up. "Her name is Valissa."

"Where is she?"

"Back in the Station."

Regina chuckled. "And here you are having sex with a woman you've never met. It seems you've already had sex with at least one of the Jnaar females. Or perhaps she was Sien'ou. It doesn't really matter. Don't you feel guilty about that?"

He lay silent for a moment, staring at the glittering ceiling. Then he spoke. "You sound just like my companion. Of course I feel guilty, but things happen." He turned his head to look at her. "I know it's not much of an excuse, but I did eat those berries."

"Yes, blame the berries." She laughed. "You men always have some excuse when you cheat on your spouses."

"She isn't my spouse. We're only engaged," he defended his actions, knowing it was a lame excuse and it made him feel even guiltier.

"Getting engaged is making a promise to be faithful to each other, isn't it?"

"You're right, it is."

"I'm only guessing, but I think you've cheated before. Once a cheater always a cheater, am I right?"

Not answering her was probably an admission of guilt, but she was right, he had cheated many times. Already on Nu-Eden. He remembered them all—Coletta Burskin, Valissa's friend; Jirina Markham, who carried his child; Leezi Ballard, Valissa's sister-in-law; Anina McClary, the doctor at Alpha Colony; Sister Angela and all her Angels. They had been nuns of all people, and Nurse Mabel, the woman his brother Ted had been involved with.

Oh yes, he had cheated. Too many times.

He didn't have to mention the Xandra and her daughters. That was before he met Valissa. So that didn't count as cheating. Strange how some things just don't work out. He'd wanted to make a new start on this planet, but so far, he'd failed.

Was it his fault? He wasn't sure if there was an answer. Yes, he had been under the influence of the Xandra. She had compelled him and everyone else to have sex with anyone who was willing. Actually, everyone was willing because of the Xandra's manipulations.

"You haven't answered my question." Regina's words interrupted his thoughts.

"You want to know if I have cheated on my fiancée? I don't know if I can honestly answer that. I've had sex with other women, but there were complicated circumstances beyond my control."

She smiled. "There always seem to be complicated circumstances with you men. Like I said, once a cheater always a cheater."

"You're wrong about that. I never wanted to cheat. Things just happened. It was never entirely my fault. I was hoping things would be different here. Once I was free of the Xandra, I wouldn't be compelled anymore to have sex with other women." It wasn't a lie.

"Who is the Xandra?" Her eyes searched his face.

"You don't know about her?"

"No, I don't."

"She's the equivalent of the Dark Goddess on the fourth planet. The Jnaar

93

brought a piece of her to this planet and created the Dark Goddess a thousand years ago. Have you been to Nu-Eden?"

She shook her head. "No. Our exploration team was sent here before the real colonization of the fourth planet began. I know nothing about the fourth planet and what happened there. Are you telling me things didn't go so well?"

There was nothing humorous about Cameron's laugh. "Not going so well is quite an understatement. Everything went wrong on Nu-Eden. Every man and every woman was changed into something not human by that alien entity. Only a few of us escaped. We came here to find sanctuary, to get free of the Xandra."

"What about the space station? What happened to it?"

"The space station is also lost."

"I don't understand."

"There are no humans left on the space station. It is controlled by the Xandra." Bitterness filled his words. "I left my brother there. He was mortally wounded when we boarded the space station to get some supplies. The Xandra promised to keep him alive, not his body but his personality, in a body she created for him. I hope we made the right decision."

"If he is alive, you did," Regina assured him.

"My brother is now a creature of the Xandra. He is a copy of what he once was. Not human, that's for sure."

"Did you know that the members of the Council are just like your brother? The Goddess created the bodies their minds inhabit now. They are practically immortal."

"They told me about that. Somehow, I see nothing but horror in it. Nobody should live so long." He sat up and looked for his clothes. His pants and shirt lay not far from him. Getting to his feet, he went to retrieve them.

As he slipped into his pants, he looked at Regina, who was watching him with a little smile on her face. She had changed position. He could see her exposed breasts and noted their nearly perfect shape. He also became aware of his semi-erect penis, realizing he was still turned on and it would take little teasing from her to make him walk back to her and have sex with her again.

"It's been quite a while since I watched a naked man putting on his clothes," she said.

"I guess I should feel embarrassed dressing in front of a woman I don't even know." He chuckled and slowly pulled his pants past his hips, hoping insanely she'd ask him to come back to her, but she didn't.

"I should be embarrassed watching you, a stranger, getting dressed."

He grinned. "We're not really strangers anymore, not after we... you know?"

She noticed him staring at her exposed breasts and crossed her arms in front of her, while resting on her elbows. "Make no mistake about it, Mr. Cameron, even though our bodies were joined for a short time sexually, that doesn't mean we are friends now. I don't know you and you know nothing about me. We are still strangers."

"Don't call me Mister Cameron, not after we've been intimate with each other. That cannot be changed. I'm Rob, but most people call me by my last name without the Mister. We're the only humans among alien people. The least we can do is be friends."

She seemed to hesitate, but then she nodded. "You're right, we shouldn't be strangers, but it takes more for two people to become friends than just having sex. Besides, it was only for a short time anyway. Not enough time to really get to know each other."

"That could be rectified," he said, his grin growing broader. He made motions to push down his pants again.

She shook her head and laughed. "Forget that notion. I should be angry with you for even suggesting that, but I think I'll forgive you, knowing that you are under the influence of those berries you consumed." She pushed herself to a sitting position, but keeping her arms crossed over her breasts, and gave him a calculating look. "Prove to me you are a friend by not staring at me when I get up. Give me some dignity."

He lifted both hands in a defensive gesture. "I promise I won't stare, but you can't stop me from enjoying the view of your naked body. And you do have a nice-looking body, if you don't mind me saying so."

"Now you're embarrassing me, Cameron. If you were a true friend you'd look away."

"Okay," he said, reluctantly, letting out an exaggerated sigh. "It's just...I like looking at naked women. Any healthy man does. There is nothing wrong with that. A woman should be happy if a man wants to look at her."

She snorted. "Typical male logic. Next thing you'll tell me a woman should be ecstatic if a man forces himself on her. After all, that's what she really wants."

"There is a difference between looking and wishing and actual touching, especially when it is not wanted. A real man doesn't do that. I don't do that. You have nothing to worry about, Regina." He turned away from her. "See, I'm not looking. You can get up and walk away. I promise I won't watch you, if that's what you want. I hope to see you again, though. Dressed. We'll both be dressed, okay?"

"Okay. See you then. I'll be leaving now."

He didn't hear her walking away, even though he strained his ears. After sufficient enough time had passed he turned around, but she was gone.

Regina was a bit of a prude, he decided. As he recalled how she had churned her lower body in his lap, he smiled. She was still passionate and even a bit wild.

Thinking about it didn't help his aroused state. His gaze took in the glassy surface of the pond and he recalled a similar pond back on Nu-Eden when he met the entity who called herself Xandra. He almost expected her to rise out of the water. He knew it wouldn't be the Xandra, but another entity like her, one they called the Dark Goddess on this planet. He had met her already, not physically but in spirit, the first time by the pond back in the tunnels when she used Carini as a channel to contact him. Carini had tried to convince him that he had been hallucinating, because he inhaled ilia-spores. Somehow, he didn't believe her, not then and not now. More than ever he was convinced now the Dark Goddess had spoken to him.

He was certain it had been Carini, who came to him in his prison and brought him to this pond, but she must have left him at some point. He had no doubts it had been the Goddess who appeared to him as Valissa. With her powers of the mind it wouldn't have been difficult for her to erase his memory of the moment when the exchange took place. Unless she hadn't been here at all and what he experienced had only happened in his drug-induced mind.

Another thought occurred to him. Had it really been Regina Seagul or just another manifestation of the Goddess? He couldn't be sure. It could have been the real Regina, but one thing was certain… it hadn't been Valissa who made love to him. How could she have been here?

Valissa, my sweet Valissa. It wasn't you, but you felt so real. Perhaps you were just an illusion fabricated by my intoxicated mind, or perhaps you were the Dark Goddess herself. It doesn't matter. For a short while I was happy lying in your embrace.

Looking at the placid water he was plagued by doubts whether Regina actually had been here. The woman who had claimed to be her hadn't given him any proof of her real identity. The Goddess could have taken all the information from his mind and played him. There was no way for him to know the truth, not at this moment.

Of course, there was also the possibility that the woman who claimed to be Regina was a clone of her, created by the Goddess, but with no awareness she was not the real one but a duplicate. Apparently, people who had been replaced didn't know they were just carbon copies of the original. That's how it had been on Nu-Eden. It would probably be the same here.

His thoughts drifted to Hunter, who had gone to another cavern. Had he been successful in locating the real Regina Seagul? Or only another clone? Too bad their coms didn't work down here. It would be much easier had there been a way to stay in touch.

Shrugging, he turned away from the pond. Then he touched the device strapped to his wrist. A three-dimensional cube expanded, showing him his location and the direction he must take to get back. He had no idea how much time had passed since his departure from his room. Time meant nothing down here where it was always daylight. There was no sun and there were no stars to record the passing of time. In a sense, time stood still. It seemed peaceful here, but he knew that was just an illusion. So far he hadn't faced any real dangers. However, he didn't doubt they existed. There was a reason why the warriors carried weapons here and in the tunnels. This was not the paradise it seemed.

Suddenly he felt naked and vulnerable without weapons. Driven by anxiety, he hurried back to the relative safety of his place of confinement.

# CHAPTER EIGHT

IT TOOK HUNTER A MOMENT TO REALIZE WHERE HE WAS WHEN SOMEONE shook his shoulder. He opened his eyes and looked at the anxious face of the Jnaar girl who had rescued him from the Dal Losos.

"Sira," he said, his voice still thick with sleep. "How long have I slept?"

She gave him a little smile. "Long enough to have made me wonder if you're still alive. I came to check on you."

He sat up, rubbing the sleep from his eyes. "I must have been really tired. Normally, nobody would be able to come this close to me without me waking up first. It gives me cause to be a bit concerned."

"Had I been an enemy you may be dead now," she said.

He doubted that. He still had Dawn who would have warned him of any danger. Obviously, his AI had not worried about his safety. His gaze fell on a fur lying beside his. He didn't remember it being there when he lay down to sleep.

Sira saw his look. She smiled mischievously. "I slept beside you for a while," she said. "When I got up, you still slept. I didn't want to wake you. Now it is time we eat. You must be hungry. Come, my mother has already prepared food. I hope you can eat the same food we do."

"I've eaten Jnaar food before," he assured her, smiling. "I'm still alive."

He followed her into the other room and found Sira's sister, Heerie, and her mother already kneeling at a low table, shallow plates in front of them.

"He's awake," the mother greeted them. "We feared your spirit may have left your body."

Hunter chuckled. "It may have left while I slept but it returned. My body needed the sleep. I feel rested now. I thank you for letting me sleep this long." It took him a moment to remember her name, but it came to him quickly, possibly because Dawn reminded him without him realizing it.

Caseera.

She gestured with her hand. "You don't need to thank us. It is Sira who is responsible for your welfare. She brought you here."

He seemed to detect a note of resentment in her words. "I don't want to cause any problems," he said, "I will leave if that is what you want."

She shrugged and motioned for him to take a place across from her. "You will enjoy our hospitality by sharing a meal with us. After that, you can decide what you must do." She threw a thoughtful look at Sira. "Or perhaps my daughter has plans of her own."

"My plans are dictated by my curiosity," Sira said. "I want to find out what it's like outside and on other worlds."

"Why? You'll never leave here to visit those other worlds," Heerie said.

"You may be right, but our ancestors came from the stars. Hunter is from the stars. He has seen things I'll never see, but I can see them through his eyes... in my mind."

"Your curiosity will be your undoing someday," Caseera warned. Her eyes turned to Hunter. "Come and sit down. It seems you'll be with us for a while. My daughter has always been a troubling and problematic child. Ever since her father was killed, she has talked about the outside."

"He was killed on the outside and I need to know more about what happened," Sira said with a heated voice.

"I've told you many times to let it rest. Nobody questions the Guardians. They are the law."

"Just because I'm a female they won't let me join the warrior clan. I can fight as well as any male," Sira said, stubbornly.

"Perhaps if you'd spread your legs for one of the Guardians you may get your wish." Heerie gave a sneering laugh.

"I won't spread my legs for any male," Sira said, "especially not for one of the Guardians. They are nothing but creatures of the Dark Goddess. Not Jnaar of pure blood, not anymore."

"Don't talk like that." Caseera spoke sharply, looking around the room.

Sira didn't answer. She walked to the table and folded her legs under her.

Hunter followed her example by getting onto his knees across from the older woman. She offered him a large bowl filled with some kind of fruit. He took one. "Stosa."

She touched her chest and smiled, obviously pleased. "You speak our language well," she said. "How would stosa sound in your language?"

"If I would say it in my language I would say thank you."

"That sounds strange in my ears. I've never heard someone talk in another language before."

"The Sras have their own language," Hunter said.

"We don't communicate with the Sras, even though our warriors have made many of them slaves. Once they are slaves, they refuse to talk," Sira said.

"You have slaves?" Hunter said, curious.

The older woman threw Sira a warning look. "We don't talk about that."

"There is much you seem to avoid talking about," he replied. "What do you fear? The Dark Goddess? The Guardians?"

"These are things we don't discuss. It is best that way." She looked at Hunter, her alien face solemn. "Now, enjoy the fruit from the fiira-tree. Aside from tasting delicious, it will also provide you with nourishment. We are fortunate to find it in such abundance nearby."

She watched him bite into the red fruit and smiled with delight when she saw his expression.

"It does taste wonderful," he said. "It's been a long time since I ate something as tasty as this." It was not a lie. He took another bite, savoring the smooth and sweet flavor. "You say these trees are growing wild and you just have to pick the fruit?"

"Yes, they grow wild, but we do have to take care of them. Old branches need to be removed; the fruit needs to be picked. We have to keep away the wild animals. Sometimes a group of Wiook invades the forest of fiira trees and we have to fight them off. They do not go easily." She laughed as if something funny had popped into her mind. "I can't blame them. They were here a long time before us. It is their world and they challenge our presence here."

"Wiook?" he repeated, remembering the monkey-like animals they had run across in one of the small cavern on their fourth day in this underground world. "We met a large party of them in the tunnels on our way to the Jnaar city. We were told they are peaceful."

"You were told correctly," Heerie said. "They are usually peaceful, but when it comes to food they will defend their right to get it. They are intelligent, maybe even a little cunning. Their teeth and claws are sharp and they can inflict painful, if not mortal, wounds. Even the warriors do not search them out to fight, especially since it is a bad omen to kill a Wiook."

"I was told that." Hunter wiped his mouth with the back of his hand, wishing for a napkin. He didn't know why he thought of a napkin, but kneeling on a soft cushion at a table in the company of three women, even if they were primitive aliens, somehow made him feel civilized.

Looking around, he saw a long bench from thin woven branches against one wall. A thick fur covered the seat, making it look comfortable. Bowls and metal pots stood on shelves. Some of the bowls held fruit and what appeared to be nuts. In the corner stood a pedestal also made from branches. A water filled basin atop it. He also saw a large urn full of water. A few cups made from burnt clay hung from hooks on the wall above the urn. Everything appeared clean and well-kept.

These people might live in primitive surroundings, but they were not savages. His eyes fell on the little cat-like creature lying on top of one of the benches. It seemed to return his gaze with watchful yellow eyes. A pet?

"Is that what you do then? Guard the fiira-trees?" he said to the three females.

"No," Caseera replied. "Sometimes we help with picking the fruit. Everyone must spend some time doing chores like that."

"What does everyone usually do besides picking fruit? Do you have duties you must perform every day?"

"Not every day. I spend much of my time teaching the young," Sira said.

"So you're a teacher." Hunter nodded. He glanced at Heerie. "And you?"

"I help take care of the Elders, the ones who live in the community shelters," Heerie said. "I'm also learning how to make bowls and other things from calla-sand."

*Calla-sand…a clay-like substance.* Dawn translated automatically for him.

"You make pottery? Interesting. Do you also mold images of animals or people from calla-sand?"

She nodded. "I'm not very good at that, but there are some Jnaar who have a talent for it. It takes lots of practice."

"Everything does. A long time ago I knew someone once, who was such an artist. She had a gift with her hands." Thinking about his ex-girlfriend Dawn brought back happy and painful memories and he suppressed them. There was no need to dwell on the past.

"Now that you know what we do, tell us something about yourself," Sira said. "What's it like on the world where you come from?"

"Well, I was born on a planet we called Emerald, a wild and untamed world. My people live on the surface, which is covered with tall mountains, huge forests, and vast savannahs. Many animals roam there and some are quite nasty, much like the Keeras while some are like the Thrall, good only for hunting and for food."

"Are you a hunter then, like your name?"

"I've hunted animals but only for sports." He paused, wondering how he could explain his job to people who have no idea what electricity was, or how modern gadgets, like the computer on his wrist, worked. People, who have never seen a light-strip or a hologram, or talked to someone kilometers away, couldn't even imagine those things.

"However, hunting wasn't my duty. My job was building things," he said.

"Like what?" Heerie looked at him expectantly, like a child waiting for a gift.

He pursed his lips, lost for words. "I put magical things into dwellings, like lights that turn on when it's dark. I installed shiny surfaces on which you could see people who were far away, and through which you could communicate with them. Things like that."

"That sounds like something the story tellers would say," Heerie observed. "Even the Guardians can't do those things, and they have great knowledge from the time when the Jnaar traveled among other worlds just the way you claim to have done."

"Your ancestors also had wondrous things like that, but you lost the knowledge when your people were stranded here on Iceworld."

Sira pointed at the computer on his wrist. "What is this?"

"That's a good question." He hesitated, remembering how young Rasar had asked him the same thing. "This is one of the many devices we use on my world."

"What does it do?"

"It helps me remember things."

"How?"

"By storing information. It never forgets anything."

"What else does it do?"

"It keeps me company when I'm alone. I can talk to it and it talks to me."

"Show us."

It was time for a little bit of truth. He hoped they wouldn't freak out.

"You heard her, Dawn," he said, addressing the AI. "Say hello."

"Hello," Dawn said.

"How did you do that?" Heerie stared at him. "You spoke with a female voice."

He laughed softly. "I didn't say anything. Dawn did. That's what I call her."

"You keep a female prisoner inside that band? How can that be?" Heerie touched the gadget gingerly, pulling her hand away almost immediately. "I felt a tingle," she said. "Is it alive?"

Hunter shrugged. "Dawn is alive, but not like you and I. She doesn't have a physical body. She's... How can I explain it? She's a spirit, real but not real."

"That doesn't make much sense," Sira said. "I think you're trying to trick us."

"It's not a trick. Let me ask you a question. Have you or anyone you know ever seen somebody who was supposed to be dead? I'm not talking about someone who was re-created by the Goddess. You know what I'm talking about?"

Caseera nodded her head slowly. "I haven't, but I've heard others telling stories about seeing spirits. There are those who claim to talk to the spirits of the dead."

"All right, this may make it a little easier. The spirit who lives inside this band will appear to you. She may look real, but she isn't. She doesn't have a real body. Are you ready for this?"

"Is this spirit evil? Can she harm us?" Heerie looked a bit scared.

"No, she isn't evil and she won't harm you. She is my friend."

"Then show us."

Dawn had obviously followed the conversation, and before Hunter could ask her to appear, she took the initiative. A foggy shape appeared beside him, took on substance, and then the image of a dark-skinned young woman sat beside Hunter.

"I'm Dawn," she said, smiling.

The three Jnaar women sat in silence. Heerie's lips formed an O, but Sira and Caseera just stared at Dawn.

"Where did you come from?" Sira finally said.

"I've always been here," Dawn said. "I'm Hunter's invisible companion."

"Not so invisible now," Caseera observed.

"That's because Hunter wants me to be visible. Like he told you, this body you see is not a physical body. It is just an illusion, not real."

"You look real to me," Heerie said. She reached across the table and tried to touch Dawn, but her hand went right through the AI's image. Hastily, she withdrew her hand, as if she'd made contact with a hot iron. "I felt something, but there is nothing there, nothing to hold onto," she said. "How is this possible?"

"We call it science. Your ancestors possessed science, probably more advanced than ours," Hunter tried to explain yet knew none of the three females would understand. There wasn't anything they could compare it with. They lacked the basic knowledge. To them this was magic.

"Make her go away," Heerie said. "She scares me."

"I'm sorry. I didn't mean to scare you, but you asked for a demonstration."

"Some things are best not known," Caseera said.

Dawn's image disappeared.

"She had black skin like yours," Sira observed.

Hunter nodded. He didn't tell her about Dawn's ability to take on any shape or skin color she chose. Caseera was right. Some things were best not known, especially the things people didn't understand.

Sometimes it was best not to reveal too much. He realized he was not among friends. Even though these females acted friendly, he knew nothing about them. Just because Sira had saved him from possible harm at the hands of the Dal Losos didn't mean she had no ulterior motives. Too much knowledge in the wrong hands could prove fatal and be turned against him. He had to be more careful in the future. The Shadow-dwellers were not regular Jnaar. They worshipped the Dark Goddess.

Looking into the luminous, almost questing eyes of the Sreel, he wondered about the small creature. There was certain intelligence in the yellow eyes that seemed to study him with uncanny curiosity. How much did this strange little animal comprehend? Was it only a pet or was it used for other purposes?

He became aware of Caseera watching him with the same curiosity as the Sreel. Touching the gadget on his wrist, he smiled. "She is not real, just a projection. You are in no danger from her."

"I believe you," the older woman said softly. She rose and adjusted her leather skirt, which had moved up to reveal her naked thighs. Even though thin, they were still smooth and well-formed. When he caught a glimpse of the dark triangle between them, he averted his eyes, slightly embarrassed to be caught looking at an older woman's sex-organ. It was enough to see Sira's and Heerie's exposed breasts while having breakfast, even though he had to admit he enjoyed the view. Both girls were young and their breasts were superbly formed.

Caseera took away the bowl with the fruit and put it on one of the shelves. Hunter rose and stood uncertain what to do. "Well, I thank you for your food," he said, "I think I'll be leaving now." He looked at Sira. "There is only one problem; I'm not quite sure which direction I have to go to get back to the hut that was assigned to me."

"It doesn't matter," Sira said. "I'd like you to stay for a while so we can talk. As I said before, I am curious about the things you can tell me."

"If that's what you wish. As long as it doesn't cause you any trouble with your elders or whoever runs your community."

"It won't," she assured him. "Even if it does, I'll deal with it."

There was a commotion from the door. When Hunter turned to see what it was all about a couple of warriors brandishing long knives stormed into the room.

"Don't move," one of them said in a loud voice, while staring at Hunter.

Hunter raised his hands in the air to indicate his surrender. "I have no such intentions," he said slowly, wondering what they wanted from him.

The other warrior looked at Sira. "You were seen bringing this spy into your house and you were heard uttering subversive words."

"Who accuses me of that?" Sira said huskily.

"We have our sources. You are lucky the Guardians are busy with other problems, otherwise you'd be taken in front of them to justify your unhealthy talk."

Hunter watched the two for signs of hostility, ready to defend himself, but they only glowered at him. "You. You'll come with us."

"Where are you taking him?" Sira demanded.

"None of your concern. Keep out of this or you'll join him."

Hunter walked ahead of the two males through the open door. Outside were four additional warriors. They carried spears with the sharp heads aimed at him.

"He didn't offer any resistance," one of the two with Hunter told them.

All four lowered their spears, but kept a watchful eye on Hunter.

"May I ask what this is all about?" he said.

"You have been found to be a spy and a hostile intruder. Don't deny it and don't try to run away again."

"Run away again? When did I run away before?" He couldn't help but chuckle. "Where would I run to? I got lost and Sira rescued me. She brought me here. Besides, I'm not a spy. I came here to find a friend. That's not a crime."

"Be silent. No more talking!" The speaker glared at him. "Now, move."

Ringed by the six warriors, he let himself be marched down the street to an unknown destination. He didn't look back, but he wondered if Sira was watching. He also wondered who had told them his whereabouts.

They left the small settlement of houses and followed a well-traveled road through a densely forested area. After about twenty minutes of walking, they entered a tunnel and followed it for another fifteen minutes or so. The tunnel finally widened and spilled into another cavern. Before they could enter the cavern, a group of Jnaar with spears stopped them.

One of them stepped up to Hunter and peered at him. "Who is he?"

"We bring you another slave," the speaker of his captors told him. "Watch him. He is a dangerous spy."

"We will take good care of him." The warrior grinned evilly. He poked Hunter with the blunt end of his spear. "What kind of creature is he? He could be a Sras; he has the small eyes, but they are dark and his skin color is strange. Is he a Sras who is suffering from some kind of disease?"

"He's not a Sras. He comes from the outside."

"From the outside? I've never seen one like him before. Are there more of his kind?"

The warrior shrugged. "I wasn't told. All I know he's considered a spy and has been deemed a slave. He's all yours." He and his companions turned and walked back into the tunnel.

The rest of the new group of warriors came closer to Hunter and studied him with curiosity. "He looks strong. We'll put him to work loosening the rocks," one of the said.

The first warrior slammed his flat hand forcefully into Hunter's back. He laughed when Hunter stumbled forward. "No need to hurry," he said, "you have plenty of time to get acquainted with your new job."

Hunter gritted his teeth, trying to stay calm. It would have been easy to hit his tormentor in the face and knock him flat and, hopefully, break his nose. He probably could have put a second one out of action by smashing his foot against his chest or head, but it would have been a stupid and useless move.

He had no illusions because the rest of them would use their spears to kill him. He had no choice but to see what developed.

"Remember this bastard for me, Dawn," he muttered under his breath. "Someday I'll want to thank him for this."

*Duly noted.* Her voice sounded ghostlike in his mind. *Don't do anything rash.*

He heard subdued voices and the familiar sound of men working with metal and stone. His assumption was proved correct when they rounded an outcropping of rocks. A group of males was standing in front of a partially carved hole in the wall ahead of them, swinging picks. Hunter could see a couple of Jnaar warriors with spears and whips. He didn't have to guess what their job was.

When he and his escorts arrived at the wall, one of the overseers looked expectantly at them.

"This one is new. He comes from the outside. Put him to work."

"Does he need conditioning?"

The warrior shrugged. "Find out. We have to go back to our post."

Receiving another violent shove, Hunter was propelled forward and almost into the arms of the overseer except a rough hand thrown against his shoulder stopped him. The Jnaar gave him a somewhat surprised look.

"You seem docile enough," he said. "Most of the new slaves don't accept their fate this easily." He looked Hunter in the eyes. "Do you understand what I'm saying?"

After a quick evaluation of the situation Hunter didn't see any advantage in keeping it a secret. "I understand you quite well," he said calmly.

"I'm surprised you do. Are you really from the outside?"

"Yes, I am."

"I've never been outside, but I've heard stories. How do you survive the time of palos? Apparently, it gets very cold."

"We live inside a giant egg where it is warm." Hunter didn't care if the Jnaar understood what he was talking about. There was no way he could explain to him in a few words what an artificial habitat was and how it worked.

"Are there many of you living inside this giant egg?"

Hunter gave a grim chuckle. "More than I can number. If I get mistreated here, my people will come and take revenge. We have terrible weapons that can throw burning flames over a long distance. Your spears are as useless against such weapons as are bare hands against an attacking Keeras."

"If you and your people are so powerful, how did you get captured?" the overseer challenged him.

"I wasn't captured. I came here out of my own free will."

"But you have been captured, despite the terrible weapon you claim to possess. You are a slave." His eyes searched Hunter's body. "Where are those weapons?"

"I came unarmed and in peace. The Shadow-dwellers are the aggressors, not I, and yet, I've been accused of being hostile and a spy."

"If you've been accused and found guilty by the Council then it is so. Now, enough talking. Get one of those pick-axes over there and get to work."

"What is my job?"

"Breaking rocks out of the wall for the smelter to make metal for weapons. What else would you be doing?" The Jnaar shook his head, obviously puzzled by Hunter's ignorance.

Hunter walked over to the indicated spot and grabbed one of the two pick-axes lying among the small rocks on the ground. Hefting it, he gave it a quick examination. The head was made from crude iron and the shaft from some kind of hard wood. It looked strong enough for the job he was supposed to do.

A number of Jnaar males were attacking the wall with their pick-axes, breaking out chunks of rocks. As they pried chunks out of the wall, the rocks fell to the ground, accumulating in small piles and making it hazardous for the slaves who worked with bare feet.

Hunter looked down at his own feet. His boots were still in Sira's house. This was not going to be fun. He hoped he could keep his toes from getting broken by falling rocks.

# CHAPTER NINE

"How long are they going to keep us cooped up in here?" Malone stood staring out of the only small window that wasn't covered up from the outside.

"It's only been three days," Cameron said, wondering the same thing. He hadn't seen Carini or the woman who claimed to be Regina Seagul since that night by the lake. Sometimes he wondered if he had actually been there or just imagined everything. Perhaps some hallucinogen in the food had caused it.

"I wish they'd at least bring us some descent food instead of this tasteless stew we have to eat every day," Malone complained.

"You won't get any arguments from me." Cameron pushed away his empty bowl and rose from the cushions where he'd been sitting. "At least they're not letting us starve. You have to give them that."

"I guess I'll have to," Malone growled. "It looks like someone is finally coming."

Cameron joined the big man by the window. Looking at the nearby jungle, he saw a slim figure coming down the narrow trail that led into the thicket. A female. As she came closer, he recognized Carini.

She looked in his direction and must have spotted him behind the window, because she lifted an arm and waved.

"I think one of us will finally be rescued," Malone rumbled.

"Rescued to where?" Cameron said, waving back.

Carini entered their room moments later. "I would have come earlier, but they wouldn't let me see you." Her smile was apologetic.

"Are you talking about the Council?" Cameron said.

"Yes, but I persuaded them to let me take you out of here for a while."

"For a while? Are we still prisoners?"

"They said you weren't really prisoners, but at the same time they can't let you walk around by yourself." She glanced at Malone. "They allowed me to take you both to see the Goddess."

"What is she saying?" Malone looked at Cameron.

"We'll finally meet the Dark Goddess," Cameron told him.

"That will be interesting. What about that woman Regina Seagul? Will she be there?" Malone looked expectantly at Carini, even though he knew she didn't understand him.

"My friend wants to know if the woman we seek will also be there," Cameron said.

She shrugged. "I don't know."

"When are we leaving?"

"Now." When Cameron went to pick up his laser, she stopped him. "Don't bring weapons. The Goddess will not harm you in any way."

"What about the warriors outside?"

"They've been told to let you leave here. They won't be a problem."

"Well then let's go and meet the Goddess."

Carini led them into the jungle and down a narrow path. It wasn't the same path he and Carini had walked days before. The jungle was thicker and the trees taller. Cameron wondered if it might hide dangerous critters, but they didn't encounter anything larger than a few furry, cuddly animals and some large dragonfly-like creatures with shimmering transparent wings. At one point, a few of them whirred around his head like a swarm of mosquitoes. When he swatted at them, Carini grabbed his hand.

"They are harmless. Don't hurt them."

"I've had painful experiences with insects similar to these on one of the planets. You're sure they won't sting or bite me?"

"They're just curious. Besides, they eat only nectar."

The path ended abruptly. Ahead of them lay a field of bright, yellow flowers. Beyond that rose two huge pillars toward the ceiling, like a doorway to some hidden kingdom. A wall of trees grew on one side of each of the pillars. Tall shrubs between the pillars restricted their view to whatever lay behind the trees and shrubs.

Carini laughed and danced among the flowers. "Aren't they beautiful?"

Cameron had to smile at her antics. "Yes, they are, but what about those two statues holding long knives in their hands? What is their purpose?"

"They are not statues. They are guards to keep anyone out who is not invited."

"You mean they're alive?"

She nodded. "But you don't have to be afraid of them. You have been invited."

"As long as they know that. We have no way of defending ourselves should they decide they don't like us." Cameron eyed the two strange creatures with suspicion. They didn't look like Jnaar or any living thing he was familiar with. Vaguely humanoid, their serpent-like heads with protruding, yellow eyes, they appeared menacing and imposing. They held long knives in three-fingered, large hands. Their fingers were tipped with sharp, curved nails, long and sharp enough to disembowel a grown man. They did not need knives and he guessed they were only for show. He wondered who they needed to impress or intimidate.

"You worry too much," Carini told him. "If they wanted to harm us, they would have done so by now."

"I'm not so much worried about you as I am about me. After all, you are a daughter of the Goddess. Surely they recognize that."

"They do, but even I am not always allowed to visit the Goddess."

"Who would want to attack her? There must be enough sentries in the tunnels to prevent anyone with hostile intentions from getting this close."

"It is not the enemy that is far away the Goddess is worried about," Carini said, ominously. She looked toward the opening between the pillars. "Come now and let us enter the realm of the Goddess."

Cameron glanced at the two large guardians who still hadn't moved. They looked like immobile statues, except for the glitter in their yellow eyes. They were watching every move he, Malone, and Carini made and could be upon them in a few long strides if they suspected a threat to their goddess.

"What is this place?" Malone wanted to know.

"We're about to enter the kingdom of the Dark Goddess," Cameron said.

"Those statues look imposing."

Cameron chuckled. "They're watchdogs, not statues, but apparently harmless."

"They don't look harmless to me. I wish we had brought some weapons. I don't like this whole thing. Everything looks too peaceful. We may be walking into a trap."

"Carini assures me we're safe. I trust her. So, come on, Malone, let's meet a goddess."

When they stepped through the shrubs, Cameron stopped for a moment and held his breath, taking in the beautiful scenery ahead of them. A small lake surrounded by trees and colorful bushes created a sense of serenity and peace. Flowers grew in abundance on the grassy areas near the lakeshore. He saw naked girls frolicking among the flowers and in the water. A number of small huts stood to one side not far away.

Carini laughed when she saw his surprise. "This is my birthplace," she said. "All of my sisters are hatched in these holy waters." She pointed to a huge floating plant in the center of the lake. "The Goddess lives there."

Not for the first time Cameron experienced a feeling of déjà vu as his thoughts took him back to Nu-Eden and his first meeting with the Xandra. He wondered what form the Dark Goddess would take when they finally met.

"Will she come on shore or do we have to go to her?"

"Only you will go," Carini said.

"How will I get there?"

"You will float across the water." Carini laughed. Stepping up to him, she put her arms around his neck and looked into his eyes. "Don't be concerned about anything. The Goddess is not evil. The Jnaar call her the Dark Goddess because they fear her. There is no reason for them to feel that way. It is the Jnaar you need to worry about. Besides, this will not be the first time you have met her." Her smile was mischievous. "She didn't hurt you then, did she?"

"Are you talking about the incident that night by the pond?"

"Yes, I am. I apologize for leaving you like that, but she requested it."

"So the Goddess was there? I didn't imagine everything?"

"She was there." She hesitated. "Maybe what I'm saying is not entirely true. Even though you saw the Goddess, it was only an image of her, not her physical body. My body was still there with you."

"In other words it was you I coupled with, not her."

"You coupled with my body but not my spirit. It was her spirit that influenced everything you experienced. It was the Goddess who brought you pleasure. She used my body as a vessel."

"How about the woman we seek? Was she there also in spirit only...or not at all?"

"I cannot answer that, because I was not present." She touched his cheek. "I will be waiting here when you come back."

"What about Malone? What will he be doing in the meantime?"

"Your friend will be looked after. Don't worry." She stepped away from him and looked across the water.

When Cameron followed her gaze, he saw something floating on the water, approaching them. As it came closer, he saw it was a flimsy contraption, obviously a boat. It was empty, and he wondered how it moved across the water.

"That thing doesn't look safe," Malone said beside him. "I'm not getting on that."

"You won't have to," Cameron told him. "I'm going alone to meet the Goddess."

"Well, good luck. Don't drown."

The boat hit the shore with a gentle thud. "Go," Carini said.

He walked toward the lake and stood on shore studying the fragile structure. It was a narrow platform with curved sides. Woven from reeds and then covered with some kind of transparent substance to make it waterproof it didn't appear to be strong enough to hold his weight. Shrugging, he jumped into the water and climbed into the boat. When it didn't sink, he looked back at Malone and Carini.

"How do I make it move?"

"You don't," she told him. "The Saphyx will pull you. Perhaps you should sit down."

Slowly the boat began to move away from shore and he sat down, not wanting to lose his balance and fall overboard. Curious, he looked into the water and saw a couple of large, dark shapes just below the surface; they began picking up speed as they headed for the floating plant, pulling the boat behind them.

The floating plant appeared bigger as he neared it. A carpet of large leaves and a mass of purple flowers covered it. The creatures under the boat maneuvered it so it came to a halt parallel to the plant-island, making it easy for Cameron to step onto the surface of the plant. The leaves and flowers felt soft under his boots and he wished he had left the boots back on dry land. He moved away from the edge, afraid he might slip into the water. Looking around, he realized the enormous size of the plant. Much larger than the one the Xandra inhabited on Nu-Eden.

He didn't see anyone and it almost took him by surprise when a soft voice called his name. Turning around, he started at the woman standing among the flowers. She was completely nude. Long, red hair spilled down her smooth, white-skinned body, partially covering her breasts. He didn't know what he had expected her to look like, but it came as a shock to see her in this form.

"Xandra?" he said, his voice suddenly hoarse.

Her laughter sounded like a silvery bell. *No, I am not the Xandra. Not the one you know, anyway.*

Her lips hadn't moved and he knew she had spoken to him in his mind. She came closer and stood in front of him. Her alien eyes glowed with green fire and her lips pulled into a mocking smile. *Is this how it happened when you first met her?* Her hand moved to his belt and began to open it.

"How do you know what happened?" he croaked, suddenly bewildered and confused.

*I know everything about you, Rob Cameron. You and I are connected the way you were connected to her. I see what you see, I experience what you experience. You cannot hide any secrets from me.*

She opened his pants and slid her hand down to his penis. Curling warm, soft fingers around it she began stroking him until he was stiff and aching for her.

"Why are you tormenting me like this?" he moaned.

*Tormenting you? That's not what I read in your mind. I know how you long for her embrace and the ecstasy you found in her arms. Ecstasy and joy you will never find in the arms of your fiancée or any other human woman. I can give you the same ecstasy.* Her lips touched his gently. Then she pushed his pants past his hips to free his erection.

With frantic movements, he pulled off his boots and stepped out of his pants. Naked, he crushed her to him. His hands cupped her full buttocks and his penis pressed into her belly. Laughing softly, she sank to her knees, pulling him with her. Then she pushed him onto his back and straddled him. Slowly, she moved her pelvis in his lap, tantalizing his searching member with her thick pussy-lips.

"Don't tease," he almost shouted, his desire for her uncontrollable.

*But that is how you like it, Rob. You want me to tease you.* Smiling, her teeth flashing white between red lips, she lifted up and molded her pussy-lips over the swollen head of his stiff penis.

He cried out from the unbelievable pleasure and pushed up. Chuckling, she went with his movement, preventing him from entering her, but then she sank down slowly, engulfing him with her soft, wet sheath.

Delirious with pleasure, he sobbed as she rode him with wild reckless-ness. Deep down he knew she was manipulating his mind, but he didn't care. She was right, he longed for the embrace of the Xandra. She was also right with her assumption that no human woman would ever be able to completely satisfy his desire. Only the Xandra could. The Xandra wasn't here, but the Dark Goddess was. He was home again.

She stretched out on top of him and kissed him deeply, feeding him her saliva. He swallowed it eagerly, relishing the taste of sweet honey. It gave him strength and stamina. Still locked together, they rolled until she lay on her back. Her legs opened wide and he moved between them with great vigor.

Time froze for an eternity as he swam in a sea of pure rapture. He forgot about the woman who waited for him inside a small artificial habitat surrounded by ice and snow, forgot his promise to her. Forgot about the real world above him. For a while he was a god in a universe where nothing else existed but the alien woman in his arms and the joy she brought him.

However, even eternity must end sometime; so must the feeling of ecstasy when the stark reality of life returns. Coming to his senses, he found himself lying on his back among the soft, purple flowers that covered the giant plant floating in a small lake in the bowels of a planet covered with a

deep blanket of snow. His memory came back with a rush and he was overcome with guilt when he thought about the betrayal he had committed.

Oh Valissa, what had he done? How could he ever forget about her? He
pledged his love to her and promised to be faithful. He'd broken that promise
too many times. How would he ever be able to live with that?

A woman's soft laughter beside him made him turn his head. "Valissa?"
He knew it wasn't Valissa.

The woman in the guise of his fiancée shook her dark-blond hair out of
her face. Her hazel eyes mocked him. "I can be her whenever you want me to
if it pleases you." Her lips moved and she spoke with Valissa's voice.

"I will know you aren't her," he said, his voice betraying his agony.

"I can change that by making you believe it is her. You will never know
the difference, except your pleasure will always be the way you experienced
in my arms when our bodies were joined." She stroked his chest with gentle
fingers. "You are different from the Jnaar whose seed I've been collecting.
They've never shown the passion you have shown me. To them, I was only
an entity to be studied and experimented with. You've given me new
emotions and knowledge to study and absorb."

Cameron laughed dryly. "Are you saying you'll be using me as a study-
object?"

"Oh no. Not a study-object. I've absorbed all the knowledge you have
stored inside you. I've taken your seed into me, and I will create a new breed
of hybrids, part human and part plant. They will not be distinguishable from
real humans, but they will be a superior species. They will leave the tunnels
and live on the surface of this planet, make it their own."

"Will they be able to reproduce? When they get old will their children
turn into a bunch of zombies, like the offspring of the Jnaar and your
daughters?"

"I have learned. They will grow old and die the way humans do, but they
will live much longer than normal humans."

He sat up and looked down at her, momentarily distracted by her appearance. "How can you know it will turn out that way?"

When she smiled, he wanted to take her into his arms and cover her face
with kisses and tell her how much he loved her. How was it possible she
could look and act so much like Valissa? It worried him. How easy would it

be for her to make him forget the real Valissa? She could make him believe anything, including his acceptance of Valissa's presence.

"Can you please change into a different form?" he said with a low voice.

"Why? I thought you'd want me to look like your fiancée. Am I wrong?"

"If you can look into my mind, you must know the real truth.

There was no malice or mocking in her voice when she spoke. "How can I know what you truly want if you don't know yourself? Your mind is complex and your thoughts contradictory. If you desire me to change, I will. Who do you want me to look like?"

"You choose, but be somebody I've never seen before."

The outline of her body shimmered; her skin became shiny and took on the substance of jelly. Her face widened, her eyes changed shape and grew larger, the color of her hair darkened. It happened with incredible speed. When her metamorphosis was done, she looked like a Jnaar female, still hauntingly beautiful and desirable, but she was a stranger.

"Is this better?" she purred, her voice silky and seductive.

He knew she was playing with his mind, perhaps even taunting him, but it didn't matter. As long as she didn't remind him of any of the women he knew and had been intimate with, he could deal with her new attempt to seduce him.

"Thank you," he said. "Perhaps now we can talk?"

"About what?"

"Carini said you wanted me to tell you about your origin. I don't know anything about it."

"You've done that already. When I joined my mind with yours, I also joined with that portion the Xandra put into your brain. It was euphoric for me to become one with a part of an entity that was like me. The Jnaar told me that they brought me to this planet, but I never really understood the implication of that until now. I am separate but also a part of something much larger. I finally know what and who I am. I am the Xandra. The knowledge you brought me has made me whole." She moved to a sitting position. Reaching out, she touched his cheek. "You will always be special to me, Rob Cameron. You are my connection to my origin."

"I'm curious about something. Are there more like you in other caves?"

"There are no others. I am the only one on this world."

"One of my people went to another cavern to find the woman we are searching. We were told it is also a home of the Shadow-dwellers. Don't all Shadow-dwellers worship you?"

"The Shadow-dwellers are descendants of the Jnaar who decided to stay mainly underground and devote their life to studying and nurturing me. That was the original plan. It isn't anymore. They have strayed from that plan." Her alien eyes looked wistful. "Some of them have stopped worshipping me."

"It is not easy to worship a god or goddess who isn't always present."

"I am always with them in body and in spirit. They can visit the temple they built in my name anytime to worship me."

Cameron studied her face and body and marveled again how beautiful she was. Every part of her body was so perfect. There wasn't a blemish on her skin.

"But you are not there. You are here."

"I am here and I am there. I am in every cavern where Shadow-dwellers live."

"Physically or just in spirit?"

"Both?"

"I don't understand. How can that be?"

"That's just the way it is. If you take a part of my body and put it into another pond or lake, it will grow, just like this one. My spirit inhabits that plant. All those separate plants are connected by my spirit. I am one entity. What happens to one happens to all of me." She smiled. "Don't forget I am a goddess."

"You may have great powers, but you're not a goddess." He spoke with conviction but wondered if he believed his own words.

How would one define a god or a goddess? She could create life. She had the ability to take on any form she wanted. She could read minds and make other life forms do her bidding with the power of her mind. She was immortal as far as he knew. What else did she need to possess to give her the status of goddess?

"Let me ask you something else. The man I told you about, his name is Hunter. Are you aware of him? Is he all right? Did he get to where he wanted to go?"

After a short pause, she replied. "He is in that other cavern and he is alive."

"Did he find Regina Seagul?"

"That he did."

"The real one or just another of your manifestations?"

"Both."

Her chuckle made him look into her purple eyes and he tried to read in them if she was serious or just making fun of him. "Am I to understand the woman I met here is not the real one?"

"I didn't say that. You asked me about the one your friend met." She laughed softly.

He shook his head in confusion. "You're not making much sense."

"It will in time. For now, just relax and let me make you feel good." With those words, she pushed him onto his back and touched his penis. Stroking it gently, she caused him to have an erection. He was suddenly aware of the sweet, intoxicating scent the flowers emitted. They made his head fuzzy and fueled his desire for her. Moaning loudly, he watched her slither on top of him. She sat astride of his body, her gaze locked with his. With agonizing slowness, she sheathed him, took him deep into her creamy softness. She smiled when he gasped for breath, unable to avert the hypnotic power of her eyes.

"You will be the father of many children," she said, rotating her lower body and squeezing his pulsating member. "They will be the forerunners of a superior race who will someday rule this world."

He reached for her and pulled her down, crushing her soft breasts against his chest. Putting his arms around her, he held her tight as he slammed into her from below. He didn't remember anything after that, only incredible bliss and ecstasy.

# CHAPTER TEN

AFTER ATTACKING THE WALL OF SOLID ROCK WITH A PICK-AXE FOR HOURS, Hunter ached in places he had never been aware of before. Every muscle on his body felt as if it suffered some kind of torture. His shoulder muscles hurt the most.

His naked toes had survived without getting crushed by falling rocks, but he discovered crusted blood on his toes and feet stemming from small cuts. He had been working with a small group of Jnaar who had ignored him the whole time, not even acknowledging his presence when he joined them. However, when their overseer told everyone to stop working and take a break, they threw curious glances at him.

"My name is Hunter," he said, trying to break the ice. "I am a stranger here."

At first none of them said anything, but by the way they looked at him, he knew they were surprised to hear him speak in their language.

One of them actually smiled. "We would have never guessed that you are not one of us," he said, chuckling. He was a big man with solid muscles. A long scar on his right shoulder testified to an injury probably caused by some sharp object that had fallen on him. He peered curiously at Hunter. "What are you? Your eyes are the eyes of a Sras, and yet, you don't look like one.

We've never seen anyone of your appearance. Even your skin is black. Did you fall into a fire?"

Hunter laughed. This was a new question to answer. "No. It is my natural color. I am a human. My people came to this world from far away. We live on the outside."

"How can you live on the outside? It is the time of palos and nobody can survive the harsh conditions on the surface," one of the other Jnaar said.

Hunter sighed. How many times did he have to explain who he was and where he came from? "We live inside a giant egg that protects us against the cold."

"How many of you are there?"

The guard had asked him the same question, but this time Hunter gave a more honest answer. There was nothing gained by not telling the truth to his new companions. "Not many."

"How did you come to be a slave of the Shadow-dwellers?"

"I came here looking for one of our females. She was abducted by them." He wiped his hand across his sweaty face. "This is hard work. I'm not used to working this hard."

The others laughed. "You will get used to it after a while."

"How did you come to speak our language? Or is this also the language of your people?"

"No. We speak a completely different language. I learned how to speak Jnaar from your people. I am friends with the Jnaar. My companion who guided me here is a Jnaar. His name is Ramuuro."

"Is he a big male?"

Hunter nodded. "Quite."

"They brought a big Jnaar before you arrived. He is part of another group of slaves."

"There are more slaves?"

"Many." The Jnaar with the scar touched his left shoulder with his balled fist. "I am Ragna."

Hunter repeated the gesture, knowing this group of slaves had accepted him into their midst. Counting seven, all of them fairly young looking, he remembered that the Shadow-dwellers captured only young males and females on their raids. "Are there any female slaves in the mines?"

"No, not in the mines. The females are used mainly for breeding, but they do other menial jobs."

"Who breeds them?"

"The males of the Shadow-dwellers. Who else?"

"Don't they have enough females of their own?"

Ragna emitted a sound that conveyed his disgust. "Of course they do. The captured female slaves are needed to bring new blood into their tribe."

"What about captured males?"

Ragna laughed. "Forget about getting behind one of their females or even one of the slaves. They don't need us. We're only good for working the mines."

"Unless the Dark Goddess takes an interest in you," one of the others said.

"That doesn't happen often. I haven't been that lucky."

"I wouldn't call it lucky. When you come back from an encounter with the Dark Goddess you may not be you anymore," said another one.

Ragna gave him a long look. "You should know, Rozzni. If I remember you were summoned once by the Goddess. Perhaps that's why you've been acting so strangely ever since. She's changed you into one of her creatures. Now you're probably one of her spies."

Rozzni stared at Ragna. "I don't know what you seem to remember. I was never summoned by the Goddess."

"There you go," Ragna said, "You just confirmed my suspicion. You don't remember because she made you forget."

"Now you're talking nonsense, Ragna." The sudden haunted expression on Rozzni's face betrayed his terror and fear they may be telling the truth. "You all know what he's saying isn't true."

Everyone looked at Rozzni for a while with serious faces, but then they started laughing. Ragna clapped him on the shoulder.

"You almost believed it yourself, didn't you?" His gaze wandered to Hunter. "You are familiar with the Dark Goddess and know what she can do?"

"I've met the Goddess," he told them. He didn't see a reason to keep it a secret. He was aware of their scrutiny and probably sudden mistrust.

"Do you remember your meeting with her and what happened," Ragna asked.

"I remember most of it. If you're wondering about me being the same person I was when I came here, I can assure you, I'm still the same."

"That is good to hear. Did you find the female you're seeking?"

"I have, but I'm not sure if she's the real one."

"You can find out easily enough. Just suck on her breasts. If sweet nectar flows from them she is a creature of the Goddess," one suggested.

"I didn't know that." He remembered one of the guards taking Laneea's nipple into his mouth when they arrived in the Jnaar city for the first time. Raaskar started to explain the reason, but he never did in detail. "It is something I'll have to remember."

Rozzni's laugh was without humor. "You'll probably never get a chance to use your newly acquired knowledge. You should have sucked on her breasts when you had the chance."

"Enough talking," their overseer shouted at them. "Back to work."

They finished the work-day in silence. It seemed nobody felt like talking. When they finally stopped working, Hunter almost dropped from fatigue. He hadn't known his body could hurt worse than before, but it did. He followed his new companions into another cavern. It was as bleak looking as the one where they'd been working all day. There were quite a few other slaves already in the cavern, many of them resting on woven mats, obviously their beds for the night.

Looking around, he spied Ramuuro with another group that was also just coming out of one of the many tunnels. Even though there were quite a few big males among the slaves, Ramuuro stood out from the rest and wasn't hard to miss

Hunter was surprised to see a number of Sras. They kept to themselves to one side of the cavern. It seemed even as slaves the animosity between the two races still existed.

"Let's go and get our food," Ragna said, probably more to Hunter's benefit than the others.

They headed for a spot in the cavern that was obviously where the food was distributed. He and his companions joined the line of slaves and stood waiting for their turn. When he came to the counter, the guard who stood behind it gave him a questioning look. "Where is your bowl?" he finally demanded.

"I don't have a bowl. I'm new here."

The guard reached under the counter and handed Hunter a bowl baked from clay. "Don't lose it. It's the only one you'll get."

Hunter shrugged. "I don't plan to hang around that long," he murmured. When the guard filled his bowl with some kind of thick, gray-colored stew, he wasn't overly impressed. Sniffing it, he made a face, hoping it tasted better than it smelled.

Even though he was hungry, the sight and odor of his supper dampened much of his appetite. "What is this stuff?"

"You may not want to know," Ragna said, chuckling. "It is nourishment, which you will need if you want to survive."

His group walked over to the wall with the mats. Squatting down, they began to eat. Hunter watched as the others scooped the stew out with their fingers. Lacking any eating utensils, he followed their example. The food didn't actually taste bad and he cleaned out his bowl, finding he was hungrier than he'd thought.

When they were finished eating, he stood. "I saw my companion with another group. I'm going to look for him." With that, he walked toward the place where he had seen Ramuuro. He had to pass the group of Sras. As he walked past them, one of them rose from his sitting position and stepped into his path. His golden eyes gleamed under his ridged forehead as he looked at Hunter.

"I am Manrah, son of Uroo. Remember me?" the Sras said, a smile spreading across his alien face.

"I remember you," Hunter said, recognition dawning in him. He had been one of the Sras they came across on the surface as they were battling two of the savage six-legged Sirkrris

"You saved my father's life," Manrah said.

"How is your father?" Hunter was shocked to encounter a Sras he knew here of all places. The chances of that happening were nearly as impossible as finding another human.

"My father is well. His leg is healed." Manrah grinned, his fangs shining white between his lips. "I am surprised to see you here. Are you a slave like us?"

Hunter nodded. "Sadly, that is the truth." He remembered to ask something else. "How is Arlee?"

"She also is doing well." Manrah pulled his ridged forehead into a frown. "She was fond of you, Darkskin."

Darkskin. Arlee had called him that. He must have left an impression with her if she mentioned it to Manrah. He had been attracted to her, but one night of passion was not enough to really get to know someone, even though her mind had been connected to his through Dawn while the AI downloaded Arlee's memory and knowledge.

"I was fond of her, too," he said. "I've been thinking about her a lot." That was not a lie. "How did you happen to end up here as a slave?"

"We came to this place accidentally while hunting for Likas. Before we realized where we were, the Glittereyes surrounded us. We were only three hunters. We fought and my companions were killed. I was taken prisoner." He spat onto the ground. "They treat us like Leeas. The food they serve us is not fit for eating. We need meat to survive and to be strong."

Hunter had to suppress a smile. "I've eaten their food and I agree with you."

"You are friends with the Glittereyes?"

"I am friends with them and with you. I take no sides."

"You are friends with them, and yet, here you are their prisoner. Perhaps you should choose one side," Manrah suggested.

"I am not friends with the ones that made me a slave. These are different from the others."

"To us they all look alike. They are our enemies." The young Sras spoke harshly, his anger apparent. "If we get the chance, we will slay them all."

"We are all slaves here," Hunter said, softly. "Not all the Glittereyes are evil. Maybe it's time to make peace with some of them, especially the ones who are also slaves. It can only benefit everyone. It is better to live in peace with each other than to constantly fight."

"You speak noble words, but when the time comes to seek your freedom you will have to kill or be killed," Manrah said.

"I try to avoid that, but you are correct, I will kill if I must." He smiled grimly. "I am not that noble when my survival is at stake."

"Will you sit with us, Darkskin?"

"I would like to, but I've been assigned to work with a group of Jnaar. It probably is in my best interest to sit with them. Also, I was on my way to talk to my Jnaar companion who was captured at the same time as I. So, please, don't feel insulted, and don't worry, I will never be your enemy."

Manrah nodded. He closed his left hand into a fist and held it up. "You and I will not be enemies, Darkskin, to that I swear."

Hunter also made a fist to seal the bargain. "I would prefer if you'd call me Hunter."

Manrah exposed his fangs as his lips formed a smile. "If you so wish, Hunter."

As Hunter walked away, he noticed the Jnaar nearby watching him with curiosity. It didn't matter. He shrugged mentally and searched again for Ramuuro. He found him standing with his back to him not far away, in conversation with a couple of slaves. It seemed his guide had not seen him yet.

Not wanting to startle the big Jnaar, Hunter called out before he reached him. "Ramuuro."

Ramuuro turned around. His face didn't show surprise when he saw Hunter. "I was wondering when I'd see you here, Hunter. We shouldn't have let them take our weapons."

"Maybe you are right," Hunter agreed, "but this is only a temporary condition. I'm not planning to stay for a long time."

Ramuuro growled deep in his throat. "I share your desire, but it may not be easy to escape here. There are many guards with spears and knives. We are not armed. I've been told they are quick about using their weapons to kill if a slave tries to escape."

Hunter made a sound that was close to the one Ramuuro made. "I've been in worse situations, my friend. Sooner or later there will appear an opportunity. Just be ready. You are wrong if you think the slaves have no weapons. They have pick-axes and probably other tools. All can be used as weapons."

"What manner of creature are you?" one of the Jnaar with Ramuuro said. "You could be a Sras but for your forehead and black skin. You are not Jnaar, either, and yet you speak our language."

"He is a human," Ramuuro answered for Hunter. "And he is my friend."

"I saw you talking to one of the Sras," the other Jnaar said. "Are you friends with them as well?"

"Yes, I am. I also speak their language, even though I'm not one of them." Hunter gave the other one a hard stare. "I hope you don't object."

"The Sras are our enemies. You can't be friends with the Jnaar and the Sras," the Jnaar said, persistent with his accusations.

"Sure I can. I have no quarrel with neither of you, unless you give me a reason." He was getting annoyed with this Jnaar.

Smaller than the average Jnaar Hunter had met so far, this one had a narrow face, which made his large eyes appear even larger and lent him a sardonic look. Hunter decided he didn't like him.

"You do what you think is right," the little Jnaar said. "Just know who your real friends are when it comes time to choose."

"My friends know that I am their friend. I don't have to prove that at every opportunity." He shifted his glance to look at Ramuuro. "I hope you don't forget where your loyalties lie, because I won't."

"I've promised Raaskar to be your guide. You are his friend which makes you mine also. I'm with you in whatever you're planning." He looked around the cavern as if worried someone might overhear their conversation. "Not all the slaves in here are what they seem. Some may be spies for the Shadow-dwellers or even the Dark Goddess. We must be careful."

Hunter eyed the little Jnaar. "Can you be trusted?"

He returned Hunter's scrutinizing look. "Can you?" With a glance at Ramuuro, he said, "I'm not even sure if I can trust him. He's been here only for one sleeping period. Now you show up, a stranger who claims to be from some race I do not know. You could be a creature of the Dark Goddess."

"I could be," Hunter said with a grim smile. "I assure you, I'm not. I come from a world far away. My people and I are stranded on this alien world. All we want is live in peace with everyone already living here; that includes the Jnaar and the Sras, especially with the Sras. The Jnaar and we are intruders to their world."

"I was born here," the little Jnaar said. "I have a right to be here as much as any Sras."

"We take that right, remember that. This is a hostile world for us humans and for your people, but we are here now. We shouldn't waste time and energy fighting each other, instead we should work together."

"Tell that to our overseers," the Jnaar said with a sneer. "They seem to have different ideas." He turned and showed Hunter his back. It was covered with welts and old scars. "This is how they treat slaves. They love to use their whips to make certain we don't forget our place and who the masters are."

The second Jnaar, who had been listening silently until now, chuckled. "If you'd keep your thoughts to yourself, Kinaar, and your words inside your mouth, you wouldn't always get into trouble."

Kinaar made a hissing sound like an angry serpent. "Just because I'm smaller than average doesn't mean I have to take being kicked and insulted by everyone." He glared at Hunter one last time and then stalked away.

Ramuuro shook his head. "He seems to have a temper."

The other Jnaar laughed. "He doesn't trust anyone. He's suspicious and thinks everyone is a spy."

"That means he can't be trusted, either," Hunter said.

Ramuuro looked to Hunter. "What are your plans?"

"I don't have any, not yet, but, as I said before, this won't be my residence for long." He turned to the other Jnaar. "You never told me your name."

"It's Marak."

"Tell me, Marak, there are many tunnels leading away from this cavern. Where do they lead?"

"Nowhere. If you think you might follow one to freedom you'll be disappointed. The only way out of here is the way you came in and the tunnel that leads to the smelters. Both are heavily guarded. You'll never make it out of here alive."

"There are many slaves. We could rush the guards."

"We could," Marak agreed. "But who wants to be the first one to take a spear through his chest or belly? You?" He shook his head. "Not a good idea. I'm afraid there isn't one slave among us who would sacrifice his life so the others could be free."

"It was just an idea." Hunter realized it wasn't a good one. He felt suddenly wary and tired. His aching body reminded him that swinging a pick-axe for hours demanded some kind of payment, most of all rest. "I'm going to get some sleep. We'll talk again later."

His workmates were already curled up on their sleeping mats. Since he didn't have a mat, he lay down on the hard ground, making a mental note to go and ask for a mat the next day. This had certainly not been a good day and it didn't look like it would change for a while.

# CHAPTER ELEVEN

HUNTER FOUND THE CHANCE TO GAIN HIS FREEDOM AFTER FIVE DAYS, BUT not the way he expected. Tired from another day of hard work, he lay on his sleeping mat with his eyes closed, when someone kicked him in the side. Wincing, he opened his eyes and stared up at the guard who had kicked him.

"Get up, you have a visitor."

"A visitor? Who?"

"What does it matter? Get up."

Hunter would have liked nothing better than kick the Jnaar in the face for adding more pain to his already aching body and for being so insolent, but he knew it would only earn him a session with the whip. Groaning, he got up and followed the guard into the next cavern.

A female Jnaar stood by the entrance. He recognized Sira. She had changed the short leather-skirt she wore when she rescued him from the Dal Losos with one even shorter, but now her breasts were covered with a narrow strip of cloth. He wondered why she had come to this place and why she brought the Sreel, that cat-like little animal, with her.

She smiled when he came closer. "I would have come earlier but they wouldn't let me." She came up to him and looked into his eyes. "I demanded to see you, because I needed to tell you about our offspring."

"Our offspring? How can we have offspring? We never—"

She put a finger against his lips. "Lower you voice. I told them the Goddess has chosen you to mate with me." With that, she pulled his head down and kissed him.

Surprised by her action, he just let it happen. She moved her lips along his neck and whispered into his ear, "I came to get you out of here. There is a tunnel that will lead you back into the cavern. Someone will be waiting for you. I brought Treegg. He will stay with you. Follow him into one of the tunnels and he will show you the hidden entrance to the tunnel that will let you escape."

"I was told there is no escape."

"Trust me, there is. Just let Treegg lead you there." She molded her body against his and kissed him again. When she let him go, she smiled. "I wish we would have had a chance to taste each other's bodies," she said with a low voice.

"I thought you didn't like males. Did I get the wrong impression?"

"Because I said I wouldn't spread my legs for any male?"

"I remember you saying that."

She laughed softly. "I never found a male who awoke my desire until now."

"I'm the one?"

"Perhaps it's because you are of a different species and you excite me." She touched his cheek with a gentle gesture. "Or perhaps I just took pity on you."

"Well, whatever your reason for helping me, I am grateful." He grinned. "If there would have been more time for us to get to know each other, who knows what would have happened. You're a beautiful and attractive female."

She let go of him. "I must go before anyone gets suspicious. The guards are watching us. Don't wait too long." She walked away without turning around.

Hunter watched her until she disappeared from view, wondering if her affectionate behavior had been genuine or if it had all been just a performance for the guards. She reminded him of Raas-ini the way she carried herself and the way she talked. She would have made a passionate lover. He was intrigued by the fact that so far he hadn't seen an ugly Jnaar female, not even one who was overweight.

Something nudged his leg. When he looked down, he saw the Sreel looking up at him with its luminous, yellow eyes. There seemed to be intelligence in those strange eyes.

"Sira told me to follow you," he said. Looking around, he didn't see any of the guards paying any attention to him. They were usually lax during the sleeping period, and there were fewer of them around. That made it a good time to try and make his escape. "There is no better time than now," he murmured. "Let's go, but I won't leave alone."

The little cat-like creature seemed to understand. It began walking toward one of the tunnels. "Not so fast," Hunter said with a low voice, "there are two slaves I will want to take with me."

When he passed Ramuuro's resting place, he saw that the big Jnaar wasn't asleep yet. He had been watching Hunter. "Where are you going with the Sreel?"

Hunter squatted down beside Ramuuro. "Don't say anything. Just come with me. We are getting out of here."

Ramuuro began to rise to his feet, but Hunter grabbed his arm and kept him on the mat. "There is something else, Ramuuro. You won't like this, but I'm taking another slave with us."

"Who is this other slave?" Ramuuro whispered.

"The Sras you saw me talking to."

"A Sras? You're right, I don't like it."

"He's my friend, Ramuuro. I can't leave him here, just like I wouldn't leave you behind."

Ramuuro stayed silent, but then he nodded. "He is a slave just like you and I. Even he deserves to be free. I cannot promise to become friends with him, but I respect your wishes."

"Good. Let's go then."

They both rose at the same time. Hunter looked for the little cat-like creature and found it waiting near the place where the Sras were resting on their mats, as if it knew about Hunter's plans. He didn't want to draw the obvious conclusion, but he had to admit it made him feel more than just a bit leery about the Sreel.

When he was close to the group of Sras, one of them suddenly rose with fluid motions and looked at Hunter. He recognized Manrah. He must have been watching him. Hunter made a motion with his head, indicating the tunnel to which the Sreel had pointed. Then he and Ramuuro began walking toward the tunnel, ignoring the Sras as they walked past him.

Hunter didn't look back, but he knew Manrah was following them. They kept on walking as they entered the tunnel. When they couldn't see the entrance any longer, he stopped and waited for the Sras to catch up with them.

Manrah eyed Ramuuro with suspicion when he was close enough. "I don't know what your plans are, Hunter, but I trust they don't involve any violence toward me."

"We have sworn not to be enemies, Manrah," he said. "There will be no violence."

"Then why are we here?"

"We are escaping."

The Sras looked suspicious again. "There is no way out of here. How do you plan to escape?"

Hunter pointed at Treegg. The little animal had been waiting patiently a few steps ahead of them. "We'll follow the Sreel. It knows a way out of here."

Manrah looked at the Sreel, his doubt clearly visible; even Hunter could easily read the expression on his alien face. "How does a Krris know this escape route? It's nothing but a dumb animal."

Hunter smiled when the Sreel made a small rumbling noise in its throat. "Apparently not so dumb. I was assured it knows the way."

Manrah stayed silent for a moment; his golden eyes flickered back and forth between Hunter, Manrah, and the Sreel. Finally, he shrugged. "Who told you all of this?"

"A new friend."

"A new friend? It seems you have many friends, Darkskin. I am one of them and I'm willing to trust you. You came to our rescue out of your own free will and you saved my father's life, and probably mine, when you killed the Sirkrris. You shared our food and you fought with us against the Maklos. Perhaps the gods sent you here to save my life again."

"Who understands the ways of the gods," Hunter mused. "They may have brought the three of us together for their own purpose, but I would suggest we don't waste any more time. We don't want the guards finding us gone and getting suspicious."

"Then let's go," Manrah said.

Ramuuro had been following the conversation between Hunter and Manrah with mild interest, not understanding a word they were saying, but he had been watching the Sras closely. When Manrah moved forward, he also turned around and began walking. The Sreel ran at a good pace and the three allies from three different races had to walk fast to keep up with the little animal. After about a ten minute fast walk, the Sreel stopped and stared at the rough tunnel wall.

"What does it want us to do?" Ramuuro said. "Climb up this wall?"

"Perhaps." Hunter searched the wall but didn't see anything that would suggest a way to escape.

The ceiling was higher at this point than in the rest of the tunnel. The rough wall rose at least 20 feet up. There was a wide ledge about five feet below the ceiling but he didn't even see a crack in the wall. On a hunch, he lifted his left wrist to let Dawn scan the wall and the ceiling. *Anything?* he thought to her in his native language.

*There is a tunnel behind this wall,* Dawn informed him.

*How do we get into that tunnel?*

*You'll have to climb the wall. A narrow opening above the ledge will let you squeeze through.*

"There is a hole past the ledge," he told Ramuuro and then Manrah.

"How do you know?" Manrah appeared puzzled.

"Perhaps the gods told me," Hunter said with a little grin.

He checked out the wall and saw enough footholds in the rough surface to allow them to climb up to the ledge. Without another word, he began climbing and found enough protruding rocks to grab and to stand on. Before long he reached the ledge. When he pulled himself up onto it, he saw the crack that ran horizontally along the wall, hidden from view by the ledge.

"What do you see?" Ramuuro called to him.

"A hole in the wall," Hunter told him. "I can see an opening," he said to Manrah. "The Krris has shown us our way to escape. I guess it isn't such a dumb animal after all."

"How do you know where the opening leads?" Manrah still wasn't convinced.

"It leads into another tunnel, which will take us out of here." Hunter was

134

getting impatient. "I'll crawl through and you two better come up here fast. We don't know how much time we have." He said the same thing to Ramuuro. Then he wormed his way through the crack. It was quite narrow and he hoped Ramuuro wouldn't find it too difficult to make it through. He might lose a bit of skin, but he was sure the big Jnaar would be able to squeeze his bulk into the tunnel behind.

The tunnel he found himself in was not large but wider and higher than the crack. He could see dim light at the other end and moved toward it. He had to crawl for only about 30 feet before the narrow tunnel ended. When he inched his body out of the hole, he nearly dropped a couple of feet to the floor of another, much wider and higher tunnel.

Once he was standing again, he called in the Jnaar language. "Come on, Ramuuro, it is safe to follow me." He hoped Manrah would not need to be told when he saw the Jnaar disappearing into the hole in the wall.

A few moments later, Ramuuro stuck his head out of the tunnel. "It seems your hunch was right," he commented as he pulled the rest of his bulk into the new tunnel.

"Is Manrah following you?"

"You mean the Sras? I heard scraping noises behind me," Ramuuro answered.

When Manrah joined them, Hunter remembered the Sreel. "I suppose the Krris didn't come with you?" he said to Manrah.

"Unless it can climb walls, it most likely stayed behind. Why? Was it important for it to come with us?"

"I'm not sure. I hope not." When he looked around he noticed that there was only one way they could go. The tunnel seemed to end a few feet to their right. In the dim light of the glow-roots, he saw only darkness in that direction. When he took a few steps, his assumption was proved correct. He encountered nothing but a solid wall. Coming back to his companions, he said, "I was told somebody would wait for us and lead us to freedom. So far everything seems to be working out. I'm putting my faith into our anonymous friends."

They began walking in the only direction the tunnel led them. It didn't run straight and seemed to wind its way toward their unknown destination. Fortunately, they didn't encounter any other tunnels that might have led them astray. After about an hour in Hunter's estimation, the tunnel ended. The entrance was blocked by a wall of thick shrubs, and when they climbed out, they stood among a forest of dense trees.

"I wonder where we are," Ramuuro said with a low voice, as if afraid somebody might hear them.

"It doesn't matter. We aren't trapped inside a tunnel," Hunter said, carefully moving through the trees, watchful of anything that might challenge their presence. The others followed him at a short distance.

Through the tops of the trees he glimpsed the bright ceiling of a cavern. When he saw the glimmer of water, he knew they were near a lake. As he left the safety of the trees, he saw movement by the water's edge and quickly stepped back. As he stood behind a tree, he watched a couple of figures walking in his direction. One was a Jnaar male, carrying a spear, and the other one a female. When they came closer, he recognized Regina Seagul. She had exchanged the flimsy outfit she had been wearing when he last saw her for a short leather kilt and a small vest, also made from leather.

She seemed to be aware of him in his hiding place behind the tree, because she smiled and called. "Come on out, Hunter. We've been waiting for you."

Cautiously, he stepped into the open, not sure if he could trust her. He didn't know if she was the real Regina or a creation of the Dark Goddess. "Who's that with you?" he said in Inglis.

"This is Ramas, my husband. You can trust him."

For a moment Hunter didn't know how to take her words. "Your husband?" he finally said.

Regina and the Jnaar stopped not far from him. She spoke to her companion in a low voice. Hunter couldn't make out what she was saying.

The Jnaar gave Hunter a friendly smile. "Regina has told me a lot about you. I was intrigued to meet you."

"As I am to meet you," Hunter said, "even though until this moment I've never even heard of you."

Regina laughed. "I wanted to surprise you," she said. Her face became serious. "Now you know why I can't come back with you. My life is here now…with my husband."

"But he is an alien," Hunter said. "Your responsibility lies with us. We are your people."

"I'm happy here, Hunter. Ramas loves me and I love him, and that is all that matters."

Hunter stared at her. "Answer me this. Are you still human or has the Goddess changed you?"

She gave him a straight look. "I am aware that she has made clones of me, but I'm the original one, the one who is still human, be assured of that."

"How can you be so sure? The Goddess could have planted that notion into your mind and you'd never know it. You may believe you are the real one when in fact you're not."

She chuckled softly. "I could let you suckle on my breasts to prove it to you. I assume you know what I'm talking about."

"I know about the sweet nectar her creatures secrete from their breasts and mouth." He threw a quick glance at the Jnaar with her. "I don't think your...your husband would approve."

"He's not the jealous type. Besides, he would understand."

Hunter shrugged. "I'm willing to believe you." He smiled thinly. "You don't have to expose your breasts. Tell me...were you the one down by the lake?"

She nodded. "Yes, I was the one." Her smile teased him. "You should have taken me up on my offer when you had the chance to make love to a real human woman. You would have found out then that I'm telling you the truth."

"I always make the wrong choices. That was probably one of them," he said, his voice tinged with sadness. She was right, it had been his chance, possibly the last one for a long time, to hold a real woman in his arms. In any case, it had been his last to make love to Regina.

She looked past him into the forest behind him. "I see you've brought friends."

He turned around to see Ramuuro and Manrah still standing in the protection of the trees, ready to bolt if it became necessary. "I couldn't leave them behind," he said.

"One of them is a Sras."

"Is that a problem?"

"Not for me. I'm surprised your Jnaar companion seems to tolerate him."

"I didn't give him a choice in the matter. I hope your...husband doesn't object."

She looked at the Jnaar beside her. "Ramas does what I tell him." She chuckled softly. "He may look tough, but he has a soft spot for me. I'm a lucky woman. He adores me."

"He may adore you, but why would he want to help me escape? I'm sure his people won't look kindly upon him."

"They may not approve of his actions, but there is nothing they will do to him. He is a member of the Council."

"I don't remember seeing him when I stood in front of the Council."

"You were met by the Guardian Council of the Dark Goddess. Ramas does not belong to them. He is a councilor of the community, but that doesn't mean he has no powers. He is well respected in the Council." She touched Ramas on the shoulder. "Hunter wants to know why you are helping him."

Hunter was surprised about her ability to speak so fluent in the Jnaar language.

Ramas nodded solemnly. "I am not in favor of keeping slaves and I don't believe it is in our best interest to have a human as a slave. Regina has spoken to me about your people, and it is my opinion we should be friends with the humans."

"That is wise decision. It is our wish also to be friends with the Jnaar, and that includes the Shadow-dwellers. However, we also chose to be friends with the Sras," Hunter said.

"The Sras are savages and they make no effort to become friends with the Jnaar." Ramas looked past Hunter, obviously looking at Manrah. "It seems you have a Sras friend."

"His name is Manrah, and I wish for him to be freed with me, as well as Ramuuro, who has accompanied me here as my guide and companion."

"As you wish." Ramas seemed to have accepted Hunter's request. "Tell your companions to come out of the forest so I can talk to them myself."

"Do you speak the Sras language?"

"No, but you apparently do. You will translate for me."

Hunter turned around to look for Ramuuro and Manrah. He found them after a quick search. He also noticed that they were not standing together but some distance from each other. It appeared they still had trust issues.

He lifted his arm and waved. "Come join me. These are my friends who will help us escape." He addressed first Ramuuro and then Manrah.

Both men seemed reluctant at first, but then they ventured into the open.

Manrah's expression was obviously distrustful, but Hunter was surprised to see the hostile look on Ramuuro's face. When he came closer, Ramuuro said to Ramas, "Weren't you with the ones who dragged me down to the mine?"

"I had no choice," Ramas answered. "I cannot openly act against the Council."

"But you are going to help us now? Why?"

"Because my mate asked me to do that."

"Your mate?" He glanced at Regina. "Are you telling me you took this female as your mate?"

Ramas gave a small chuckle. "Why does that surprise you?"

"She is an alien. Not of your people."

"You are not the first one who observed that." Ramas turned his attention to Manrah, who had been watching with apparent trepidation. "I know you can't understand me, but you don't have to fear that I will betray you. You may go with Hunter. I will help you." He looked at Hunter. "Can you tell him that?"

Before Hunter could speak, Manrah said, "I understand. You...help Manrah." He spoke haltingly, searching for the words. "Manrah...grateful."

It wasn't only Hunter who was surprised. "You speak Jnaar?" Ramas said.

Manrah's fangs gleamed as he opened his mouth in a smile. "No speak... only little. Understand more."

"Good." Ramas seemed to accept it quicker than Hunter. "You must trust me. No harm will come to you." The gaze of his eyes switched to Hunter. "I have a few warriors who are loyal to me waiting nearby. They will accompany you out of here. You won't be able to make it on your own." He turned away and let out a warbled cry.

There was movement in the trees farther away and then a group of warriors came out into the open. They were armed with spears, but they carried them with their points down. Hunter counted a full dozen warriors and wondered why they needed so many.

Glancing at Manrah, he saw him going rigid, and he couldn't blame him. It wasn't easy to stay calm while watching a dozen armed warriors approaching and having no weapons for defense should the need arise.

Ramas must have noticed Manrah's reaction because he held up a hand. The warriors stopped advancing. "I promised no violence," he said to

Manrah. "I will keep my promise. They are here only for your protection. You are safe."

Manrah relaxed but kept his eyes on the warriors as they came closer.

Regina came up to Hunter and smiled. "When you get home tell everyone that I'm happy here and not to worry. Perhaps someday my husband and I will come and visit you. Everything is possible."

"I suppose it is. There is one more thing," Hunter said, "what about our packs? We can't leave without them. In addition, I could use some footwear. Walking on the hard ground of the tunnels will ruin my feet for sure. I left my boots at Sira's place."

"Oh, yes, Sira. She's the one who told me about your incarceration. It seems you left not only you boots but also quite an impression with her."

Hunter felt almost uncomfortable when he saw Regina's mocking smile. "Believe me, nothing happened between us. I just slept in her house. I got lost after I saw you and she rescued me."

"Whatever happened between you and her isn't my business, but she told me all about it. In fact, she did bring your boots and I had someone get your things. You may need your weapons once you're back in the tunnels. The tunnels are not safe." She made a sign with her hand.

One of the warriors left the group and came closer. He carried a couple of packs, one on his back and another one in one hand. Hunter recognized them. When he saw his rifle tied to his pack, he felt quite confident about finally getting away from this place. He swore to himself that once his advanced weapon was back in his possession, nobody would take it from him ever again with or without his permission.

The warrior dropped both packs in front of Hunter and walked back to his companions.

"What about my boots?" Hunter asked.

"Somebody will bring them. Be patient." She looked toward the trees. "There she is."

Hunter recognized the young female walking out of the forest immediately. There was no mistaking her shapely figure. When he saw her in the mine, she had worn the same short leather skirt but had covered her breasts. This time her breasts were bare. She carried his boots in one hand.

Walking up to him, she came close and smiled. "I thought you might need these," she said so low only he could hear. "I should have insisted you come to my home and get them yourself. After you paid your debt to me for rescuing you, the way I'd planned in the first place, but Regina didn't think it was a good idea. Too bad, because I like you." She lifted up to plant a kiss on his lips. Then she whispered, "Be careful and don't trust everyone. Not everything is as it seems. Keep alert and your weapons at the ready."

She put her arms around him for a moment and held him, and then she turned and ran back into the forest. He looked after her, wondering about her cryptic words.

He looked at Regina. "When do we leave?"

"Now," she said. Her lips pulled into a little smile. "As soon as you put on your boots."

He chuckled and slipped into his boots, feeling much better immediately. Then he reached for his pack and shouldered it.

Ramuuro came and picked up his pack. "They didn't bring me my spear," he said to Hunter.

"You can have mine," Ramas said, offering his spear to Ramuuro.

Ramuuro didn't hesitate. He took it from Ramas and hefted it to test its balance. Apparently satisfied, he looked at Hunter. "I'm ready."

"So am I. Manrah, we leave now. Sorry, I don't have a weapon for you."

Manrah shrugged. "I was promised no violence. I don't need a weapon."

Hunter felt a little uneasy when the warriors ringed them, but then he relaxed. They were here for his protection. Had they wanted to kill him and his companions, they would have done so by now…before they gave them weapons. He threw one last look back at Regina as they marched away.

She waved. Ramas stood beside her, a solemn expression on his face.

# CHAPTER TWELVE

THEY LEFT THE CAVERN OF THE DARK GODDESS BEHIND WITHOUT AN incident. Hunter breathed a sigh of relief when the tunnel walls closed around them. The chance of somebody challenging them was reduced to nearly zero. If anyone would have questioned them, it would have happened while they were still in the cavern.

"This is not the way we came," Ramuuro said to Hunter suddenly, suspicion in his voice.

"I know," Hunter said. "Perhaps they know a shorter route to your city."

Ramuuro looked back at Manrah. "What about him? Is he coming with us all the way?"

"Unless we come across a tunnel that leads to his village I see no other choice."

"He won't be welcome. There will be problems."

"Let's not worry about that right now, Ramuuro. I want to get as far away as possible from the cavern. I'll be feeling much better once we've lost our escort and are on our own."

"Are you worried about them turning against us?" Ramuuro kept his voice to a murmur.

"I don't believe so, but Sira told me to stay alert, and that made me wonder. It is possible we might still run into an ambush."

"Perhaps that's why they took a different tunnel? Possibly to avoid such a chance?"

"It is possible." Hunter increased his pace to catch up with the leader of their escort. "I don't remember using this tunnel when we came to your village."

"You are correct, you didn't," the Jnaar warrior told him.

"Any particular reason you chose this one?"

The warrior turned his head to give Hunter a level stare. "I don't like to be questioned."

"I meant no harm. We were just wondering." Hunter returned the Jnaar's look. "I don't believe you like me."

"You are correct, again."

"Then why are you helping us?"

"I'm following orders. It doesn't mean I have to like you."

"Why don't you like me?" Hunter persisted. "I have done nothing to give you any reasons to hate me."

"You are an outsider and an intruder," the warrior growled. "You are friends with the outcasts and the Sras. They are our enemies."

"That's perhaps because nobody ever tried to become friends with them. They are not so much different from the Jnaar."

"They are an inferior race and not worthy of our friendship." His voice dripped with contempt. "Your Sras friend cannot be trusted. He will cut your throat when you sleep."

"I trust him with my life if need be. He and I are blood-brothers." It wasn't exactly true, but Manrah and he had shared meat and more than just one drink that night around a campfire, which had created a special bond between them. Not to mention that he was Arlee's cousin, the Sras girl who gave herself to him in one long night full of passion and bliss.

"Then you are my enemy also." The Jnaar spat out the words, causing Hunter to be wary and wondering why he was so hateful.

Dropping back, he joined Ramuuro. "I don't think he likes me very much," he said to Ramuuro. "Watch your back, my friend." He gripped his laser tightly, finding assurance in holding it. Their spears would be no match against his weapon, should they decide to harm them. For some reason, he couldn't get himself to assume they would, even though their leader had made it quite clear that he didn't have any love for Hunter and Manrah. He even seemed to hate Ramuuro, who was a member of his species, but he had called Ramuuro an outcast.

It was nearly evening according to Hunter's clock, when they came upon a small cavern. A narrow stream of water ran along one wall, providing them with fresh drinking water and a chance to wash. There was a spot empty of shrubs and other vegetation where the Jnaar warriors set up camp. Hunter and his two companions moved away from the stream and chose a spot near a clump of tall shrubs. It seemed Manrah had decided to tolerate Ramuuro, possibly even trust him, because he stayed close.

The Jnaar warriors had small satchels strapped to their hips, in which they carried food and other supplies. Hunter rummaged around in his pack and removed a couple of food-rations. Knowing that Ramuuro carried his own food, he only offered a ration to Manrah.

"It tastes bland," he said with a smile. "However, it will give you energy."

Manrah accepted the small package and watched Hunter to see what he did with it. Hunter used his teeth to rip open the outer wrapping. Then he waited for the package inside to expand and warm up. He had chosen simulated steak and potatoes and he hoped Manrah found it edible.

The young Sras followed Hunter's example. Watching the package expand, he was in obvious awe. He sniffed at the food and grunted. Carefully taking a tiny bite, he grunted again. Then he smiled.

"This tastes better than Sirkrris meat," he said. "You have wondrous things, Darkskin."

"I'm glad you like it. Remember my name is Hunter. Call me by my name."

Manrah took another bite from the fake meat and nodded. "If you wish."

"That water looks refreshing," Ramuuro said. "Do you think it would be safe if we washed our bodies?"

"I wouldn't mind that myself." Hunter watched as the Jnaar warriors knelt in the stream and splashed water into their faces and over their shoulders. "But I suggest we don't all go in at the same time."

Ramuuro rose and waded into the stream, keeping his distance from the warriors. When he came back out, Hunter removed his boots and shirt and walked to the stream. Leaving his rifle on land, he stayed near the edge when he stepped into the water. It felt cool and he wished he could take off his pants and immerse his whole body, but he knew it might turn out to be fatal. He felt jittery and on edge, almost as if he expected something to happen, but the Jnaar warriors didn't appear to even pay any attention to him and his companions.

Manrah went into the water after Hunter came out. Either he trusted Hunter to keep watch or he didn't worry about anything, because he stretched out and lay in the water for quite some time. When he came back out, his long hair was plastered against his head and his golden eyes seemed to glow. He gave Hunter a wide grin.

"I haven't been able to do this since I was captured by the Glittereyes," he said. "My body feels clean now. So does my spirit."

"I wish I could say the same," Hunter murmured more to himself than to Manrah.

The young Sras pulled his ridged forehead into a deep frown. "Something is troubling you. What is it?"

"I don't trust the Glittereyes," Hunter told him.

"You have a reason?"

"No, just my guts and the words the female who brought my boots said to me. I want you to be on guard. Since you don't have a weapon, I will give you my knife so you can defend yourself should you have to do that." He unbuckled the belt with the sheath and the knife and handed it to Manrah.

After strapping the belt around his waist, Manrah removed the knife from its sheath and studied the long, shiny blade. "It looks thin."

"It may be thin, but it is sharp and strong, so be careful. Handle it with care and don't slice off your fingers," Hunter warned. "It will never break, so you don't have to worry about that."

Manrah's eyes rested on the laser-rifle. "You have magical weapons, Hunter. Unbreakable knives and sticks that throw lightning bolts. You don't have to be afraid of anything."

Hunter smiled. "My weapons don't make me invincible. I can still be killed or overcome in my sleep."

Highly unlikely, not with Dawn alerting him to possible danger but not impossible. A rock thrown at his head from a distance or an arrow in the heart can easily kill him. So would a spear in his chest. He didn't tell Manrah that, even though he trusted him.

Hunter volunteered to take the first watch. He sat cross-legged near the protection of a shrub, listening to the soft murmuring of the stream, but he still couldn't relax. The Jnaar warriors didn't seem to worry about possibly being attacked while they slept. They didn't even have anyone on night watch. Perhaps that was a good sign.

When it was time to catch some sleep himself, he shook Ramuuro awake. His Jnaar companion woke up instantly when Hunter touched his shoulder. "Any problems?"

"None, but don't let that fool you. Be alert." He moved to a better spot. "Dawn," he whispered before he settled into a comfortable position on the moss-covered floor. "Keep watch for me. Wake me at the slightest sign of possible danger."

*Don't worry, Hunter. I've been on guard ever since you left the cavern. I detect no immediate threats. Go to sleep.*

He still lay awake, but he must have fallen asleep, because the next thing he became aware of was Dawn's urgent voice inside his head. *Open your eyes but don't move!*

Opening his eyes, his vision showed nothing but the water of the stream in front of him. Then he heard shouting. Moving his head a little, he saw someone lying not far away with the shaft of an arrow protruding from his chest. At first he thought it was Ramuuro, but then he realized it was one of the Jnaar warriors.

When he made a move to sit up, Dawn's silent voice warned him again. *Lie still.*

*What is happening?*

*You've been attacked. They already killed two of your guides.*

*Who are they?*

*Jnaar. There are many of them.*

He wondered fleetingly about Ramuuro and Manrah. They didn't seem to be anywhere. *Where are my companions?*

*Manrah is lying in the bushes behind you and Ramuuro joined the fight. He took your laser.*

"Damn!" Hunter cursed. *He doesn't know how to use it, the fool.*

*No, he doesn't. He already found that out, but he is using it as a club.*

Hunter groaned. A laser rifle was not a club. *When did this whole thing start?*

*About ten minutes ago.*

*Why didn't you wake me?*

*I didn't know about the attack until someone shot you with an arrow from a blowgun. You were lucky, the arrow only grazed you, but enough poison entered your bloodstream to immediately knock you out. It took me this long to neutralize the poison in your system. Had you received the full dose you'd be dead now.*

*So why are you telling me not to move? Am I paralyzed?*

*You are fine now if not a little disoriented for a while. They think you're dead. Let them believe that. I'll tell you when it is safe for you to move.*

Listening to the hoarse shouting and the sounds of battle, he itched to join the fight. Lying motionless and not even knowing what was going on, just didn't feel right.

*Danger! Move now!* Dawn's urgent voice inside his head made him roll out of the way.

He saw a large figure looming over him, felt the thud as a spear was thrust into the ground where he had lain. He kicked up with his feet and registered with satisfaction when he connected and heard the surprised bellow of his attacker. Twisting around, he tried to rise and was hit with a wave of dizziness. He managed to stand, but swayed on unsteady legs.

The Jnaar warrior he faced had let go of his spear, but now he held a knife in one hand and was ready to plunge it into Hunter's chest. Before he could finish his move, a dark shadow sprang at him and pushed him away from Hunter. Dropping his knife, his hands went up to his throat. Through a dizzy haze, Hunter watched the crimson spray gushing from the warrior's slashed throat, painting his clutching hands and his chest red.

Strong hands grabbed Hunter and pulled him into the safety of the shrubbery. As his head began to clear, he recognized his rescuer.

"You were right, Hunter. Your knife is sharp," Manrah said. His lips curled to expose his fangs, lending his face a savage expression. "I thought you were dead, but then I saw you move."

"I did nearly die from a poisoned arrow," Hunter told him. "I'm happy to see you alive. What happened?"

"I can't really tell you much. The Glittereyes who came with us were rising from their sleep, when a large group of warriors appeared. They shouted something and the leader from our group shouted back. My Jnaar is not good enough to understand when they speak fast, but I believe he said, "I will not break honor." Then they began fighting."

"It seems I misjudged our guardians," Hunter said. "I wonder when I was hit with that arrow. It must have happened before the attackers entered the cavern."

"I can't tell you. When I looked at you I saw you lying without moving."

"I wish I could have helped in the fight." Cautiously, Hunter peeked around the shrub and saw warriors locked in battle. Some faced each other, making threatening moves, some wrestled on the ground, while others kicked with fists and feet. Some even fought in the water.

One of the warriors looked back. He seemed to have seen Hunter, because he left the skirmish and rushed toward Hunter. It was the leader of their guardians. He was bleeding from superficial wounds, but otherwise he seemed fine.

"They want you dead, but I will not allow them to kill you," he said.

"Who wants me dead?"

"Does it matter? You and your companions must leave now. My warriors and I will hold them back until you are gone. Then we can stop fighting."

"Why are you risking your lives for us? I thought you hated us?"

"I have made a promise. Now…go!"

"My friend is among the fighting warriors," Hunter said. "I won't leave without him."

"I will call him and send him to you." He went back to join the battle. Hunter heard him shouting something to another warrior, who left his spot to look among the fighting men. Then another warrior stepped away from the mass of fighters and stumbled toward Hunter. It was Ramuuro. He carried the laser rifle in one hand, like a club.

"We are leaving," Hunter called.

Ramuuro grinned. "I was just beginning to enjoy myself."

"That's good, but we must leave now."

Ramuuro moved forward again, but then he suddenly stumbled; his body went rigid for a moment and his expression froze on his face. Pitching forward, he collapsed onto the ground. The laser flew from his hand and slid toward Hunter. An anguished cry escaped Hunter's parched throat as he stared at the shaft of an arrow still vibrating in Ramuuro's back. Bending down to pick up his rifle, he switched on the power-button and searched for the warrior with the bow. When an arrow sailed past Hunter, barely missing him, he located the shooter. With an angry roar, Hunter pressed the firing stud and burned the warrior before he could release another arrow.

Searching for another target, he didn't know who was friend of foe. Someone shouted, "Hunter, let's go."

When rough hands grabbed his arm, he turned to see who dared to intervene and glared at Manrah's anxious face.

"You had your revenge," Manrah said, almost gently. "Now we have to leave."

*He's right. You must leave now,* Dawn urged him silently.

Hunter nodded. He had enough sense to get his back pack and registered only barely that Manrah picked up Ramuuro's pack. He followed his Sras companion, who seemed to know which way to run. The cavern wasn't large and it took them only seconds to enter one of the tunnels. Manrah didn't slow down and ran with full speed down the tunnel. Hunter could barely keep up with him.

When they finally stopped, he was out of breath and gasping. "Where are we going?" he said between gasps.

"To my village," Manrah told him.

"How do you know we're in the right tunnel?"

"Because the cavern back there was the one were the Glittereyes surprised us. That's where we fought them and lost. I will never forget that." Manrah's voice sounded calm, but Hunter read the sorrow and anger in the words. Losing friends is not something easily forgotten.

"How far is it from here?"

"Maybe five sleeping cycles, depending how fast we travel." Manrah's face was solemn. "I am sorry about your friend. He died bravely."

"That he did," Hunter agreed, "but his death was useless and served no purpose. It leaves me wondering who wanted us dead and why."

"You will never know, but we are alive and that is important. Now we must move, in case they send warriors after us. We will come across another small cavern with many tunnels leading away. That's where we will lose them, but for now we cannot rest."

"Are you forgetting about my stick that spits arrows of light? I can kill them all." Hunter heard the savageness in his voice and told himself he needed to control his emotions.

He knew killing those warriors wouldn't make anything right. It would only put Regina in jeopardy. She and her Jnaar husband freed him and there was a good chance they would have to answer for that. So he just gritted his teeth and followed Manrah.

It was as Manrah had said. Seven tunnels led into the cavern. The tunnel they chose split again into three tunnels, with a few side tunnels at irregular intervals. Anyone pursuing them would surely get lost in the maze and would give up the search. When it came time to rest, Hunter was exhausted, but he was quite certain they were safe.

On the fifth day, they reached the village of the Sras. The cavern wasn't much different from the ones he had seen until now, except he found the glowing crystals in the ceiling not quite as bright and sparkling. The huts of the Sras were strung along both sides of a narrow river. They were not as sophisticated as the homes of the Jnaar. The walls were made from tall, bamboo-like poles and dried grass covered the roofs, but they were a welcome sight.

As Hunter and Manrah walked toward the village, they came upon a group of young Sras who greeted Manrah with great enthusiasm. They gave Hunter curious looks, but he didn't detect any hostility in them, especially after Manrah introduced him and told them how Hunter helped him escape from the Glittereyes.

Manrah led Hunter to the river where another group of Sras were bathing and playing games. From the number of youngsters and females he saw, he assumed they were probably mothers with their children. When they came closer, a few of the females turned to watch Hunter and Manrah approach. Suddenly, one of them let out a cry and ran forward.

He should have expected it, but it still came as a surprise when he saw Arlee.

She came up to him and stood in front of him, her beautiful face lit up with a happy smile. Touching his chin, she said, "Hunter, you found me again." Then she slapped his cheeks gently to show her deep affection.

All he could say was, "Arlee," and then he took her into arms and covered her face with kisses. When he let her go, she laughed and pushed him away with gentle force. Taking his arm, she pulled him down to the river.

His breath caught in his throat when he looked at the little boy playing in the sand. Turning his head, the boy looked at Arlee and smiled. His golden eyes sparkled under his ridged forehead as his black little arms reached for her to be picked up.

Arlee held him out to Hunter with a happy laugh. "I named him *Darkskin* after his father."

Hunter took the little boy and held him in his arms. "Darkskin," he whispered. "My son."

# CHAPTER THIRTEEN

"It is difficult to imagine that all this was covered with so much snow just a few months ago." Valissa Ballard looked up at the rolling clouds. "I wonder if it is going to rain."

Naomi Lewis shrugged and bent to pull a blade of grass out of the soft ground. Putting it between her lips, she chewed on it. "I hope it won't rain for a while. I hate the thunder and lightning the rain usually brings."

Valissa sighed and touched her belly. "I don't mind it so much, but I think he is a little afraid sometimes."

Naomi laughed. "How do you know it will be a boy? Besides, you're just beginning to show. How far are you along now, anyway?"

"I'm in my fourth month."

"In your fourth month? That tiny thing inside your belly isn't even aware yet. How can it be afraid of anything?"

"I don't know. I just have a feeling he is. As for me knowing it's a boy. I just know."

"Have you asked what Wong prefers? Does he want a boy or a little girl?"

"Len doesn't care. As long as the baby is healthy."

Naomi gave Valissa a sidelong glance. "What about Rob? He won't be happy to find you pregnant with another man's child?"

"Rob isn't coming back. He's been gone for over a year now. He probably died in those tunnels underground," Valissa said, bitterly.

"Weren't you two engaged to be married?"

"We were." Valissa stared into the darkening sky. "He promised to protect me and then he left in search of a woman he didn't even know."

"I can't blame you for being bitter." Naomi reached out to touch Valissa's arm. "I'm not going to judge you, but I would have waited. He was a good man. Handsome, too."

"He shouldn't have left me alone," Valissa said, stubbornly.

"What if he does come back? Are you still going to marry him? Will he want to marry you now that you got yourself pregnant by another man?"

Valissa stared at her friend. "Why are you asking me all these questions, Naomi?"

"Well, I've been thinking lately about our situation here and I've been listening to some people's conversations. The consensus is that if we want our colony of humans to flourish, we have to forget about such institutions as marriage. What they are actually talking about is the marriage between one man and one woman. To keep the gene pool from going stale, one woman should have children from different men and the men should have children with different women."

"So what are you saying?"

"I find that quite interesting and it makes a lot of sense." She gave a small chuckle. "It would be exciting."

Valissa tilted her head, noticing the sudden rosy color creeping into Naomi's cheeks. "Who are you planning to fogg?"

"I'm not planning anything. Just saying. Anyway, don't put it so crudely."

"Come on, Naomi. You're talking to me. I know you pretty good by now. Who is it?"

"If you really must know, Jerry's been pursuing me."

"Jerry Kullman? He's 35 years old and you're 21. He's too old for you. I thought you and Sigmund were an item. He's closer to your age and he's much nicer than Kullman, who can be pretty gross sometimes. I don't care for his crude jokes."

"I think he's funny and always in a happy mood."

"He's loud, and I don't like him much."

"Sure he's loud, but he has more life in him than Sigmund."

"Sigmund is nice and good-looking to boot."

Naomi heaved a deep sigh. "Yeah, he's that all right, but he can be boring sometimes. I need a bit of excitement."

"You think Kullman can give you that?" Valissa shook her head. "I don't know what to say. My advice is be careful, girl, and don't let whatever itches you make you do something you may regret."

"Like you?" Naomi's expression was challenging.

"What do you mean?"

"You got yourself knocked up by Wong. How different is that?"

"Much different. I was lonely and Len kept me company. It happened and I have no regrets." She looked at Naomi, her eyes wistful. "You know, it was Sigmund's mother who suggested that about men and women having different partners. She said it to Rob and me when we were still in the shuttle the first day we landed."

"It seems you took her advice." Naomi smirked. "When Rob comes back you can still have children with him. That'll be mixing the gene pool."

"That's not the reason I'm carrying Len's child. I fell in love with him."

"Do you still love Rob?" Naomi blurted out.

"How can I answer that, Naomi? Perhaps I still do, but he's not here and I have no illusions about him coming back. I'm assuming he's dead and I have to go on with my life. Should he still be alive and come back someday, well… then I have to deal with it. I'm not going to waste my time worrying about that possibility."

"You're right. Time is too precious. I'm sorry about pestering you with this. I didn't mean to make you feel uncomfortable. You're my best friend and I care about you." She gave Valissa a hug. "What do you say we'll go down to the lake and see how far they got with that boat they are building?"

Valissa laughed, happy about changing the subject. "You mean trying to build?"

"I think they'll get it built. Jerry showed me the plans and it will be a nice boat. Large enough to maneuver across the sometimes high waves, at least that's what he told me."

"Jerry showed you the plans, huh? I have a feeling there is more going on between you and Jerry than you're telling me." She held up a hand when she noticed Naomi's discomfort. "I don't want to know, unless you need to tell me."

Naomi stopped walking and looked at her hands. "I think I'm pregnant, too."

"What?" Valissa stared at the other girl. "Jerry?"

Naomi nodded. "I'm afraid so."

"How did that happen?"

"You know how it happened," Naomi said with a little smile. "We had sex."

"Are you okay with him getting you pregnant?"

"I'm not sure."

"Does he know?"

Naomi shook her head. "No. Nobody knows. You're the first one I'm telling. I'm afraid to tell my father, and Sigmund will be devastated. He actually loves me."

"You can always have a kid with him the next time."

"I could but I'm not sure if I will. I don't love him."

"Perhaps you should forget about love. Perhaps we all should. Like you said before, to keep the gene pool mixed up we have to change our accepted way of life. This is a new world with new mores and laws. The old ones are outdated and haven't much value here."

"Do you really believe that, Valissa?"

"No, I don't, but we may be forced to change our way of thinking. Let's face it, we don't have many choices when it comes to men, and I'm positive the men feel the same way when it comes to their choice of women. You may even have to have a child with Dr. Bonnet. Who knows?"

Naomi made a face. Then she put two fingers under her nose to indicate the small, square mustache Bonnet sported. "Mathematically speaking," she said with a nasal, high voice "it may rain tomorrow and it would be a good day to father a child with you, young lady. It would be my first but your fifth child. I'm surprised you chose Dr. Renaldo before me."

Valissa broke into a happy laughter. "You're pretty good with your impersonation. You should become a comedian."

"Oh, I forgot you also have a child with Professor Tennenboum," Naomi continued still using the nasal voice of Bonnet. "Actually, I am a bit disappointed you chose him ahead of me. He could be your grandfather. By the way, you are a fine addition to our stable of child-producing females. Humans will survive." Joining in Valissa's laughter, she became suddenly serious. "I wish we would have never become colonists. I was happy on Earth, but I hate it here. This is a boring life we lead."

"It is, Naomi, but this is our life now. We have to make the best of it. You and I will be the first new mothers on our new home planet. My parents left Earth because they wanted to get away from the large corporations and start a better life somewhere else. We children didn't have much choice except to accompany them. Nu-Eden seemed like an ideal world, but I wasn't happy. Had I not met Rob, I don't know what would have happened to me. I followed Rob to Iceworld, trying to get away from the influence of the Xandra, just like everyone in our group. I wanted to get away from my parents, as much as I loved them."

"Why?"

"They were drowning me with their rigid religious beliefs, especially my father."

"I gather you're not religious?"

"Not much. You?"

Naomi shrugged. "Not really. My father always said if there were any loving gods they would not let people suffer the way they do. He was very bitter when my mother passed away. She was only thirty-five, much too young to die."

"That is young," Valissa agreed. "You remember that alien entity on Nu-Eden, the one who called herself Xandra, she claimed to be a goddess. Perhaps she was one, because she changed most of the humans into her creatures. She had awesome powers, I can attest to that."

"We weren't long enough on Nu-Eden to experience that. Do you think planets are alive and everyone has its own spirit? Perhaps that's what this Xandra was. The spirit of Nu-Eden." Naomi screwed up her face. "That makes me wonder. What if this world has a spirit like that? Primitive people might call it a god or goddess."

"I've never thought much about that. Anything is possible."

"You see, maybe a few thousand years ago our home world was alive, but the spirit of Earth died. Humans plundered Earth for centuries and used up all the minerals and life-giving elements by extracting them from her physical body. Before the discovery and development of modern power sources, they pumped all the oil out of the ground, draining Earth's lifeblood and burning it in dirty, smelly engines that powered their vehicles on the ground and in the air. Can you imagine the polluted air the people must have been breathing? It's a wonder humanity survived that terrible time."

"It is difficult to imagine," Valissa agreed. "Maybe that's why Earth is as overpopulated as it is now. The Earth God has died and now there's nobody to control anything."

"Do you think there's a spirit like that on this world?" Naomi shuddered.

"So far we've seen no evidence of that. If there is one, then she probably lives underground. It's too unpleasant on the surface." She stared at Naomi, a sudden dreadful thought popping into her mind. "You may just be right about your hypothesis. If this planet has the counterpart of the Xandra then she most likely lives underground. In fact, I remember Rob mentioning something Dr. Roland told him." She slapped her forehead. "How could I have forgotten?"

"Don't keep me in suspense," Naomi said.

"According to the aborigines of Iceworld, an evil entity lives underground. She created weird, ugly monstrosities that roam the tunnels. They call her the 'Dark Goddess'."

THE END

## THANK YOU FOR READING

Did you enjoy this book?

Tell the world and leave a review at the site from which this book was purchased.

## DID YOU KNOW THAT LEAVING A REVIEW...

- Helps other readers find books they may enjoy.
- Gives you a chance to let your voice be heard.
- Gives authors recognition for their hard work.
- Doesn't have to be long. A sentence or two about why you liked the book will do.

## ABOUT THE AUTHOR

Herbert Grosshans lives near Winnipeg, Canada. He spends much of his free time spinning tales about imaginary worlds and the strange creatures inhabiting them. His first published story "The Anniversary Gift" appeared in *Sweet Revenge* published by Midnight Showcase. Even though he writes in other genres, his love is Science Fiction. He enjoys building alien worlds and societies. Most of his stories contain an element of Erotica. To this date he has published 28 books with Melange Books, not including this one. Please, visit Herbert's websites and blogs to find out more about him and his writing.

**Websites**: fictitioustales.weebly.com
**Blogs:** hegro.blogspot.com
hergros.blogspot.com

**Pinterest:** pinterest.com/herbertg
**Facebook:** facebook.com/hergros
**Twitter:** twitter.com/hergros

**Operation Stargate**
Codename Salamander

**Web of Conspiracy Series**
Death of a Hero
Traitors and Patriots
Tarnished Valor

**Mysteries**
Bullet of Revenge
Mark of the Cobra

**Novels**
Orola
Orion

**Anthologies**
Dual Visions
Tapestry of Dreams
Time Flares

www.ingramcontent.com/pod-product-compliance
Lightning Source LLC
Chambersburg PA
CBHW052137170626
46812CB00004B/1476